I0742155

OTHER BOOKS IN THE ADVENTURES OF DUKE LAGRANGE

BY JAY KEY

How to Pick Up Women with a Drunk Space Ninja

(Book I)

How to Win at Pit Fighting with a Drunk Space Ninja

(Book II)

How to Save the Universe with a Drunk Space Ninja

(Book III)

How to Battle Giant Monsters with a Drunk Space Ninja

(Book IV)

The Adventures of Duke LaGrange Omnibus, Volume I: The Collected Adventures (Books I-III)

HOW TO SAVE THE UNIVERSE WITH A DRUNK SPACE NINJA

THE ADVENTURES OF DUKE LAGRANGE, BOOK III

JAY KEY

To Finley, may your imagination take you to worlds as yet undiscovered.

Our most precious resource is hope.

QUEEN JOE

CHAPTER 1

T'CKUVU PRIME

THE LIGHTS OF T'CKUVU Prime could be seen from any other planet in the T'ckuvu System; it was a testament and a symbol to the economic boom that the planet had experienced over the last twenty cycles. From orbit, even the keenest observer would be hard pressed to find a solitary patch of rock or grass or water or anything natural. It was an industrial sphere created by business dealings and inflated interest, floating amongst its more imposing but far less colorful brethren. Of course, in Prime's case—"Prime" being the colloquial title used on the planet itself—the business dealings were all shady, the inflated interest was all maliciously manufactured, and the economic boom was another phrase for takeovers by too many criminal syndicates to count. The cloud-piercing structures springing up out of the metallic jungle and neon sea of Prime could not mask the grim reality of the planet's foundation: bloodthirsty, egotistical, megalomaniacal crime lords and gang bosses. It was both a gorgeous visualization of what beings could accomplish with grit, determination, and ingenuity, and a grimy cesspool of malice, cruelty, and greed.

Surprisingly, Duke LaGrange didn't care too much for T'ckuvu Prime. Even he had standards.

The Nova Texan bounty hunter and his Japanese-Irish ninja companion, Ishiro'shea, had been on the planet for roughly a week and were no closer to their goal of locating Ishiro'shea's parents. On the positive side, there had been no major advancements by the universe's most wanted fugitive, Admiral Lothario LePaco, and his following of bureaucratic battalions known as the Four I's—Intergalactic Infrastructure Improvement, Incorporated. During their frequent communications with Queen Joe on Kelt, there had been no evidence of a single sighting of LePaco's salmon-colored spacecraft with the license plate that read "Mister Macho." Nor had there been any sightings of Duke's former lover, the assassin Mazilda Cloax. Nobody had been able to confirm whether she had even survived the Battle of Kelt; but Duke had a hunch that she was still alive. Until it was discovered that she was actually an accomplice of the admiral, this uncertainty would have been a pretty hard pill to swallow; now he was hoping that his hunch was wrong.

Duke and Ishiro'shea had spent their time on T'ckuvu Prime investigating the whereabouts of Ishiro's parents, but they had produced no worthwhile results. They had arrived with no leads and, a week later, they were still without hope. They did their best to avoid attracting the attention of the crime bosses, so brothels and casinos were out of the question, much to Duke's chagrin. The bounty hunters stuck primarily to the establishments that were known throughout the cosmos as the most trusted fountains of knowledge and wisdom and a haven of loose-lipped unknowing informants—the bars.

T'ckuvu Prime's list of bars was lengthy and unrivaled in the sector. There was a drinking establishment for every type of consumer—from dingy and discreet dens to celebrity hangouts to refined lounges for the sophisticated drunkard; and every type of theme or fetish—from a bar that catered to left-handed accountants to one that only served liquids derived from planets that have four moons to a particularly eccentric pub that required its patrons to chase every drink with the Zylantian treat of never-ending mayonnaise. Despite sampling the unique array of alcoholic delicacies of T'ckuvu Prime, it had been an entirely fruitless enterprise. Except for the juice bars.

"Are you sure we haven't been down this one before, Ish?" Duke complained. "These alleys are starting to merge together."

The mute ninja shook his head with certainty.

"I don't see much down this way, little buddy. Anything from the Queen?"

Ishiro'shea shook his head again.

"You know, I still can't believe they found the Four I's main manufacturing planet. Finally a win for us good guys. I was hoping we'd get some more updates on that by now. And, of course, it's in the Tardasio System. You think Sol brokered anything in that deal?"

The ninja didn't respond, his focus solely on the narrow concourse in front of them.

"I bet he did," Duke mumbled to himself.

They traversed the alley, and the deeper they journeyed, the less they were showered with the electric lights of advertisements and marquees that littered this particular district. The corridors grew so dark that it was almost hard to tell that they were still on T'ckuvu Prime, which wasn't an easy effect to achieve.

Ishiro'shea stopped and pointed up at a dilapidated sign that hung by a single chain from a brick wall. It read "Booze."

Simple yet effective, thought Duke.

Under the sign was a shallow recess, within which was an unremarkable door. The door was beaten up pretty badly but Duke wasn't sure if the dings, dents, and bruises were from the natural wear and tear of time or from the crashing heads of patrons that were no longer welcome at the establishment. There was no handle.

"I guess we just... knock?"

The Nova Texan tapped the door gently with the back of his index finger.

Nothing.

He repeated the action with slightly more force.

Nothing.

He then rapped it with a fist.

A wisp of air grazed Duke's nose, causing the bounty hunter to jump back into the alleyway. Ishiro'shea, equally as close to the falling debris, did not move a single muscle, remaining in place with the poise of a statue. The sign hit the ground and splintered into pieces of various sizes. The chain swung back and forth, continually clinking against the wall.

The door opened slightly, enough for the occupant of the bar to speak without being seen.

"What do you want?"

The voice was aged and gruff, lathered in a lifetime of drink and bad decisions.

"What do you want?" the voice repeated.

"Excuse me, my good man," Duke began, "my colleague and I were in the neighborhood and were looking for a place to enjoy a drink or two. Your fine establishment sprung to mind. We..."

"Nope."

The door shut with a jarring twang.

"That went well," Duke said to Ishiro'shea.

He knocked again. The door opened again, still only slightly ajar.

"Just in case the door being slammed in your faces didn't get the point across... go away!" the voice roared.

"Is this not a bar?" asked Duke.

"It is."

"So why can't we come in and have a drink? That is what typically occurs in a bar," the bounty hunter replied smugly.

"Not this bar. I drink in this bar. A few select folks can drink in this bar. But not you, I'm afraid. Goodbye."

Duke's boot prevented the door from closing.

"Old timer, can we at least chat through this?" pleaded Duke. "We aren't here to cause trouble, we just want a drink."

The man was still not visible despite Duke holding the door open with his foot. There was no sign whatsoever of light within the establishment.

"Your foot being in my door says that you aren't opposed to some trouble," countered the mysterious doorman. "Feel free to go and register a complaint with the authorities if you wish. I'm sure they'll show you a lot of attention for such a heinous act."

"What are you doing in there that's so secretive?"

"Maybe this is an exclusive club of local celebrities and VIPs. And you, as far as I can tell, don't mean anything to anyone of consequence. So, you can go now."

Ishiro'shea tugged Duke's arm and motioned back toward the main drag.

"No, wait a second, Ish. He's lying through his teeth, if he has teeth. Are you a racist? Don't feel like serving drinks to an Earther and a Nova Texan?"

The force on Duke's boots lessened immediately.

"Nova Texan, you say?" the man asked, his tone now inquisitive.

"Yes, Nova Texan."

"Haven't met someone from there in quite some time." The voice softened, as if he was talking to himself. "Earthers, on the other hand, I see them all the time. But Nova Texas. Interesting."

"So can we come in and have a drink?" asked Duke. "It would be an honor. I don't think I've ever had so much trouble getting in to a bar."

The voice didn't reply but the door swung open to reveal a pitch-black hallway.

Duke looked at Ishiro'shea and shrugged. "We've gone into darker places."

"Are you coming or not?" howled the voice behind the door. "If you are, hurry up, and shut the door behind you."

Duke and Ishiro'shea ducked beneath the dangling chain to enter the lightless concourse.

"I wonder if they have any good happy hour specials."

CHAPTER 2

THE TRUTH, IN MODERATION

THERE WAS A LIGHT AT the end of the tunnel, or in this case, the corridor. It wasn't a particularly nice bar but it had a few places to sit and, as the sign claimed, booze. Duke and Ishiro'shea wiped away stagnant dust that had collected on the barstools and took their seats. The counter was worn and not overly clean, likely one step above failing inspection.

So far, so good, thought Duke.

The doorman walked behind the bar and tied an apron around his waist. He was a burly humanoid, barrel-chested with forearms the size of most Earthers' legs. His face showed his age; cracks made barren tributaries around his nose and mouth. Despite his advanced age, it was clear that he had been a handsome man in his youth. Strands of silver hair covered his head and matching stubble dotted his jawline.

"What'll you have?" he said, his back to his newest patrons.

"Dealer's choice," responded Duke.

The man plucked two bottles from below the bar, removed their caps, and slid them over to the bounty hunters. His knuckles cracked with every movement.

"Local brews. Good old-fashioned ale. Would rival anything they brew over on Glyptodia, I reckon."

"That's high praise, old timer," Duke responded.

He and Ish inhaled the beer. Duke choked. "Wow. That's... that's different," he coughed. "Are you sure you meant *Glyptodia* Glyptodia?"

"Yeah," the man snarled.

"I think they may have made some advancements in brewing technology since you last ventured out there, my good man."

"Or you're a giant pansy that can't handle a man's beer. Probably prefer a martini, eh?"

Ishiro'shea chuckled under his breath but all Duke could do was think about the Queen's famous martini. Even this calloused throwback would have to admit the tastiness of that concoction. Duke took another sip.

"Better the second time around," he replied, trying to save face.

"Right, stranger."

Duke and Ishiro'shea continued to down the T'ckuvian ale, one cautious sip after the next. Only a few customers were present in the single room: two T'ckuvian locals sat in a dimly-lit corner, a pint-sized Broan occupied the barstool closest to the far wall chomping on snack nuts, and another customer was asleep on the floor. Duke couldn't pinpoint the heritage of the downed drunkard, nor could he confirm that he was just asleep.

Best to let sleeping or possibly deceased unidentified aliens lie, thought Duke.

"So tell me, gents, why were you so eager to visit my humble dive here, even after I made it clear that I didn't want your business?" asked the bartender.

"Yeah, what was that all about?" replied Duke. "Who refuses business? Especially on T'ckuvu Prime."

"I do. And that will suffice for now."

"Anonymity, now that is *very* T'ckuvu Prime," responded Duke.

The bartender leaned in, his forearms resting on the uneven counter. "I repeat, why did you guys want to come in here? I don't think you're food and drink critics for the *Prime Gazette*. I don't owe anyone as much as a single damn T'ckuvian credit. I'm paid up on this place. I'm paid up on taxes. I haven't killed anyone in cycles."

In cycles?

"I'm sure you run a clean operation here," said Duke. "And we damn sure aren't in the bar and restaurant review ring. That racket is beneath even us."

"Then why *are* you here? Why were you so adamant about coming in?"

The incessant nature of the bartender's questioning placed the bounty hunters in a quandary. Duke didn't have a suitable cover and mentioning their true mission was risky. What if this crotchety old drink peddler was aligned with a crime lord? That would essentially guarantee his hatred of bounty hunters and would likely make him a tad curious as to why these two strangers were braving the urban minefield of T'ckuvu Prime to find two missing persons. Or, even worse, what if he had a partnership with LePaco? It was a stretch, admittedly, but LePaco's reach was not only wide but also diverse when it came to associates and accomplices.

The truth it is, then, concluded Duke. *In moderation, of course.*

"We've been on T'ckuvu Prime for some time now," Duke began.

"What's some time? A few cycles?" questioned the bartender.

"No, more like a week."

"Oh." The old man looked unimpressed.

"Hey, it's a dangerous mission that we're on," Duke fired back.

"I'm sure. Did a little girl lose her precious kitty cat? Is it up in a tree?"

"You done, old timer?"

"Go on."

"We're here to find someone. Rather, two people."

"That's not all too uncommon on Prime. People are always looking for someone here. What did these two people do? Murder a family member? Steal some cash?"

"No, we're not after them in *that* manner. We're trying to save them."

"Religious missionaries, then, I presume."

Ishiro'shea entire body pulsated in silent laughter.

"No, definitely not. More likely to be a restaurant critic," Duke replied.

"Then what? What are you saving these two poor souls from?"

"They're on the run and being heavily pursued by a really nasty man."

"This planet has a surplus of nasty people."

"This isn't your ordinary gang thug. This is Admiral LePaco. You know that name?"

The bartender grabbed two more bottles of ale from under the bar. He placed them under Duke and Ishiro'shea's noses.

"Yes, I've heard of Admiral LePaco," he snapped. "Who hasn't? How far from civilized space do you think Prime is?"

"Well, LePaco is back and now has a pretty impressive force at his fingertips. They're causing some major problems and trying to take over the universe."

"So I've heard," the bartender responded.

"You have? Great. Then you understand our situation. We were sent here on good intel from a reliable source, suggesting that the two people that we are trying to locate are somewhere on Prime. They're both from Earth. Probably around your age. Ish, show him the photo."

Ishiro'shea pulled out the photograph of his parents and showed the bartender.

"I'm guessing these are your parents?"

The ninja retracted the photo.

"Why would you say that?" asked Duke. "How could you even say that? He has a mask on."

"He looks just like them. Let me guess, Earthers. She's Japanese. He's Scottish. No wait, Irish. Yeah, definitely Irish. That makes you, well, a very interesting person, huh? Not a lot of Irish and Japanese hugging each other these days, right?"

The bounty hunters looked at each other.

"I'll take it by your silence that I'm right. So why are these two so important?"

"I'm not sure that's any of your business," Duke snapped.

"Fine, fair enough," the bartender replied diplomatically. "I learned a long time ago not to press people on this planet. The majority of the time, ignorance is not only bliss but it's what separates you from a *dead* you."

"We've been to almost every bar on Prime and no one knows anything," said Duke. "We're hoping that you can change that—and I'd say we're off to a promising start."

"Searching the bars first, smart move." The bartender raised a bottle of beer. "But I haven't seen them. I've seen Earthers come through, there's a huge transplant population here. No shock, right? But I haven't seen these two. Are you sure that you can trust your source?"

"It hasn't failed us yet," replied Duke.

"It?"

Duke debated for a moment whether it would be prudent to explain the nature of the astral anomaly produced by the magic orb that the Neprians referred to as the Orb That Controls Everything and Must Be Respected. He decided against it.

"Yeah, 'it.' It's not into gender identification," stammered Duke.

"Right," replied the bartender.

He's not buying that, Duke concluded.

"If you wholeheartedly trust this source of yours—"

"We do," interjected Duke.

"Right, well if you do, then I can only offer my sincere good luck."

"Thanks for the help. And thanks for the local brew. What do I owe you?"

"On the house."

"Really?"

"It's been a while since I talked to a Nova Texan."

"Free beer for being a novelty?"

"I'm sorry if that offends you, stranger."

"Not at all, I wish every place had that policy."

"What's your name, if you don't mind me asking? If I see another Nova Texan in my bar, I'll ask them if they know you."

"Duke LaGrange. Adventurer. Trailblazer. Poet. A true man of the universe. They might not know me, but they'll have heard of me."

Ishiro'shea's eyes rolled back.

"Is that right?"

"And this is Ishiro'shea. Of Earth. But you know that."

"And he doesn't speak?" asked the bartender.

"He can, at least, I think he can. He swore a vow of silence until he's reunited with his parents."

"Honorable. Don't see that much these days," the old man stated. He turned to face the ninja. "I really wish that I could help you, my mute friend."

It was the first time that the grizzly barkeep seemed somewhat likable.

Ishiro'shea placed the photo of his parents on the counter and extended his hand over the bar. The bartender shook it.

"Good luck, Duke LaGrange and Ishiro'shea..." He trailed off as something caught his eye. He picked up the photograph and examined it closely.

"What is it? Do you recognize them after all?" said Duke, his optimism unguarded.

"No."

"Oh."

The bartender sat the photo down and tapped part of the image of Ishiro'shea's father.

"But I know what *this* is."

How did this nameless owner of a ramshackle old bar in an unlit alley on T'ckuvu Prime come to know about Ishiro'shea's father's necklace?

"What *what* is?" asked Duke, feigning ignorance.

"The necklace. Or rather the pendant that he's wearing. Your pops must run with some pretty ritzy crowds, Ishiro'shea."

"I don't understand," replied Duke.

"That flash of jewelry right there is as old as this planet. Maybe older. It was stashed away on Earth. Japan, I'm guessing. It was said to be a magic pendant that helped a brave samurai save his peoples back on ancient Earth. No one knows where he got it, or how he got it. I thought it was locked away in some museum vault. But there it is. Unless it's a replica, of course."

"Probably just a replica," said Duke quickly.

"It's priceless."

At that moment, before the last syllable in "priceless" was finished, the two native T'ckuvians approached and sat on either side of the bounty hunters. They stood as tall as a Jungafallowian, their shoulders extending above where their head rested. It wasn't unreasonable to think that the T'ckuvians evolved to meet the planet's growing need of thugs and street toughs. These guys were big, ugly, and didn't come across as scholastically-minded types.

"'Allo there," the orange T'ckuvian belted. The stench of fermented grain was overwhelming. *Did this guy drink the beer or bathe in it?*

"Yeah, 'allo there from me too," echoed the purple T'cku-vian. "Where are you twos from? Not from here, I see."

"Why do you say that?" asked Duke.

"First off, you don't look like us. Second, I ain't never seen 'ya. Third, and this is the real kicker, you're drinkin' in *this* dump."

The orange T'ckuvian cackled wheezily at the purple brute's joke. The bartender ignored the comment and placed two mugs of ale in front of the locals.

"I need better clientele," said the barman.

"This place isn't that bad," countered Duke. "I prefer a nice local dive bar with a set of esteemed and classy regulars."

He raised his glass. The T'ckuvians did not reciprocate.

"My name's Roller," said the purple T'ckuvian. "This here's Noot."

"'Allo again," added Noot. He scratched the tiny patch of straw yellow hair on the top of his head. "Welcome to Prime."

"Obliged," replied Duke.

"Did we hears you sayin' that you have something priceless that needs findin'?" asked Roller.

"We didn't say anything about anything being priceless. My good man here did," replied Duke, pointing to the bartender.

"He's right," responded the crusty bartender "I did say it. But I'm right. It's quite an artifact. And to think it could be somewhere on T'ckuvu Prime."

The two brutish T'ckuvians exchanged glances and deep-throated laughs.

"Dare I ask what's so funny?" Duke queried hesitantly.

"Artifacts is a fancy word for something that's fancy," answered Noot.

These guys are brilliant.

"And we love findin' fancy things," finished Roller.

"I see. Well, my new friends, I think we have this one under control. No need for any more investigators," replied

Duke diplomatically. "But we do appreciate your offer to help."

The two ogres shared another chuckle.

"You ain't hearin' right, stranger," began Roller. "We ain't offerin' to help you find this thing."

"I apologize for the confusion. Boy, do we look silly," said Duke, raising his glass.

"What we are doin', though, is beatin' you senseless and takin' that artifact back to the boss for a payday," finished Roller.

"Is that so?" Duke said.

He stood up and drew his laser revolver, but a sharp pain pierced his hand. Then he didn't feel his gun anymore. The bartender had knocked the pulse pistol out of Duke's clutches with a bottle of the local beer.

Ishiro'shea swung at the bartender, but he dodged the strike. The blade stuck momentarily in the shoddy material of the counter. The barkeep whipped his apron off and wrapped it around Ishiro'shea's head before the ninja could respond. Noot grabbed Ishiro in a vice-like bear hug.

"No point in squirmin'," bellowed Noot. "You ain't goin' nowhere."

Duke turned around and was met with the purple fist of Roller. He hit the floor with a loud crash. Before he could regain his bearings, he felt the pressure of a giant hand grasping the back of his neck. He was whipped up onto his feet in a flash.

"Don't be thinkin' 'bout that other gun neither," threatened Roller. "I won't be pullin' my punch if you do."

That was him pulling his punch?

"Take him to the boss then?" asked Roller.

"I don't care. Do whatever you want," replied the bartender. "This is your show, gents, not mine. But leave their weapons here with me, if you don't mind."

Duke looked up at the grizzled barman through an already swelling eye.

"On second thought, you're an ass and this bar isn't a 'nice local dive,' it's a..." Duke struggled for the right insult, but the pain from being coldcocked and his genuine anger at being deceived by the bartender left little room in his brain for creativity. "...place that serves crap beer."

The bartender smiled. "I'm sorry to hear that, Duke LaGrange of Nova Texas."

CHAPTER 3

HEFTY AND THE BOOZE MAN

"WE'VE SURE BEEN GETTING CAPTURED a lot, little buddy," Duke noted. "If it's not a bunch of cave-dwelling Neprian rebels, it's Psitakki guards at an imperial gala; if it's not at the Grand Shaman's party, it's at a dumpy bar on T'ckuvu Prime by two moronic goons."

"You're the one with your hands tied. So maybe youse are the moronics," replied Noot.

"Yeah, we're the 'moronics,'" said Duke, rolling his eyes.

"I'm glad you agree with us," remarked Roller.

Two more T'ckuvians entered the room. Both were the same color as Roller.

"These the two guys with the artifacts?" one asked.

"They don't have 'em but they can help us find 'em. It's one of their daddy's necklaces, and daddy is hangin' out somewhere on Prime."

"How'd we know that?" asked one of the new natives.

"Sources," replied Noot. "They've got sources. The Booze Man thinks it's the real deal."

The newcomers looked over Roller and Noot; then they turned their attention to Duke and Ishiro'shea. They didn't seem all that impressed.

"What'd he say again?"

"Priceless," responded Roller, with a slight twinkle in his eye.

"Good. You follow proper protocol bringin' these guys in?"

"Yeah," began Roller, "we did it like we was told. Bagged their heads 'till we got here. Tied 'em up. Didn't cause any major damage. You can see they're in one piece."

"And you says the Booze Man thought this was a good score?"

"Yeah, we done told you that," replied Roller agitatedly.

"Fine. Let's go see the boss then."

The boss' quarters were as lavish as one would predict a leader of an underground crime syndicate's to be; except this was T'ckuvu Prime and there wasn't anything "underground" about it. At first glance, Duke couldn't tell if this was part of a private residence or part of a multi-floor commercial campus, but then it hit him.

Casino.

Nothing aboveboard happened in the back room of a casino, especially when that casino is located on T'ckuvu Prime. And double-especially when that back room of that casino on T'ckuvu Prime is owned by the extremely wealthy and equally extremely merciless gang boss, Hefty Senchax, leader of the Senchax Crime Syndicate.

"So you're Duke LaGrange? I've heard of you, ya' know," belched the portly crime lord, who was lounging on a burgundy plush velvet sofa. "I thought you'd be bigger."

I thought you'd be smaller, the bounty hunter mused. *Then again, everyone's smaller than you, you obese bastard.*

"I'm sorry to disappoint you, Mr. Senchax," he said aloud. "It's an honor to meet you, though I'm not exactly sure *why* I'm meeting you."

The rotund Senchax attempted to reposition himself on his velvety throne. It was clear that the overweight criminal wasn't going to fit comfortably in *any* size chair, save for that of a Mega-Troll, and he needed the sofa to account for his excess girth.

"According to my associates Noot and Roller here, you may have a lead on a priceless artifact."

Duke glanced back to see the T'ckuvian thugs grinning. They seemed to be generally proud of themselves.

A servant hoisting up a silver platter passed Hefty's couch. Hefty snatched a few morsels from the carrier, something in a shell. He slurped down most of the contents; the remainder slid over his multiple chins and settled on the front of his dress shirt. Another servant quickly replaced the one hawking the shelled delicacy; this one carried an assortment of skewers sporting a variety of brightly-colored vegetables and fruits from across the galaxy. He picked one of the skewers up with his meaty thumb and index finger and examined it closely. He then tossed it to the side of the room. The server was horrified. Hefty's fist crashed down on the plate, sending it to the floor. The server sprinted to the back of the room. Before the plate ceased its wobbling, another servant was already on all fours cleaning up the mess.

Must be watching his food intake, thought Duke.

Hefty turned his attention back to the bounty hunters. "As I was saying, Noot and Roller claim that you know the whereabouts of something that I might find valuable. And, as much as I trust their infinite wisdom, I also verified this with the Booze Man. It seems that you two may have met him at his fine den of delightful drink."

"Yes, we did. Seemed like a nice enough guy at the time. I guess we were wrong."

"So tell me about this trinket that's supposedly worth more than all of my businesses—every one of them entirely legitimate if anyone asks, by the way—put together and multiplied by seven."

"We aren't looking for any *thing*, we're looking for two people," explained Duke. "And I think your informant might have a drinking problem, because whatever he thinks that necklace is, it's not. No way it's worth that much."

"Is that so?"

"Yes, it's so."

"Why do you think he said that to me, then? Do you think he lied to me?"

"I'm not saying that," Duke stuttered.

"Then what are you saying, Duke LaGrange?" questioned the bulbous boss. "Better yet, how about you tell the Booze Man directly to his face that he's wrong?"

A figure stepped from a dimly-lit recess in the far corner of the room.

"Long time, no see, fellas," he said, acknowledging the bounty hunters. He respectfully bowed to Hefty Senchax.

"These guys here tell me that you're mistaken," said Hefty. "That this necklace isn't worth my time and effort. And I should let them just waltz on out of here."

"Mr. Senchax, it is up to you if you want them to waltz out of here but I can assure you that the necklace is worth as much as I say it is. The pendant that's affixed to it is no ordinary pendant. It's the Heart of Nobunaga."

It was obvious that Hefty Senchax and his menagerie of assorted goons had never heard of the Heart of Nobunaga. It was also clear that Duke LaGrange had never heard of the Heart of Nobunaga. It was even more clear that these facts frustrated the Booze Man.

"Is that good?" asked Hefty.

"Very. It's very good, sir. The Heart of Nobunaga belonged to the man responsible for bringing Japan out of certain despair following one of Earth's great world wars."

"Which one was it?" asked Hefty.

"I'm not sure, I always get numbers thirteen through eighteen confused. Anyways, from the darkness and devastation, Japan rose to prominence, led by a great warrior and leader, Takeo Nobunaga."

I think Ishiro's related to that guy, remembered Duke.

"Nobunaga had an item—an inexplicable and unimaginable item—that helped him defeat his enemies and rebuild his nation in a new image. Over time, the artifact that aided him was lost, found, lost, found, lost, and eventually faded into legend. Scholars just chalked up Japan's rise to charismatic leadership and slightly superior weaponry. The Heart was eventually found again. But, under the assumption that it was just a benign piece of metal, it was displayed in a museum as nothing more than a good luck charm."

"So it's not?" asked the gang leader, repositioning his mounds of blubber.

"I don't know. Not definitively. There's a strong belief that it's more than that. That it really was unimaginable. The legends and tales of Takeo's unbelievable deeds were all a product of the Heart. That's what the Irish believed. You could even say that this pendant laid the foundations for the Nipponese-Gaelic Wars."

"And this little guy's folks jacked it and sped off," Hefty hypothesized.

"That's one possibility," the bartender replied. "I'm not sure. I'm only sure that the pendant in the photograph is the Heart of Nobunaga."

The obese crime lord fiddled with his countless chins that descended like a waterfall from his jawline. He shut his eyes.

Is he thinking or did he just fall asleep?

"Boss?" asked Roller.

"Shut up, I'm trying to think," Hefty replied.

He opened his eyes. "Here's where I'm at on the matter. These two, aside from being bounty hunters—which is a massive strike against you, by the way—they don't know where this man and woman are. Therefore, they don't know where the Heart of Nobunaga is."

"True," responded the Booze Man.

"And do you think they know anything more than we do at this juncture in time?"

"They likely do not," answered the bartender.

"This is an easy one, then. We kill them. We look for this artifact by ourselves. We get it, sell it, and then turn our attention towards Admiral LePaco."

Duke's attention perked up at the mention of LePaco, particularly the prospect of him being killed by Hefty's men.

"Wait..." Duke began. Then a massive T'ckuvian hand reached around from behind, covering his mouth and transforming his plea to a muddled mess of grunts.

"You're going to die at some point, LaGrange, why not now? Act like a man," said Hefty.

"If I may," the bartender interjected, "could I speak to you privately for a moment?"

"Sure," replied Senchax. "Noot, Roller, you two make sure these bounty hunters don't escape. If they do, you're not going to want to know what'll happen to you."

The Booze Man approached the gang boss, leaned in and started to whisper. Duke couldn't make out any of what he said, but Hefty nodded incessantly and Duke could read his lips. They seemed to mouth "I see," and "Interesting," frequently.

The bartender stepped back with a bow. He returned to the shadowy location from which he had first emerged.

"It seems that I have some new, interesting information. Very interesting, in fact."

So you mouthed, thought Duke.

"Duke LaGrange, his odd sidekick man, you two are safe. For now. It seems that our mutual friend, Admiral Lothario LePaco, has a sizable award posted to anyone that provides intel on your whereabouts. I'm sure that reward will be exponentially increased if I actually have you in my custody."

"Boss," began Noot, "I thought we hated LePaco. Why we helpin' him?"

"My poor, ignorant Noot," Senchax started, "we *do* hate LePaco. More than anyone. His clean-up committee is not exactly friendly to those in charge of operations like that of yours truly, despite everything being legitimate, of course. Myself and my friends need that Four I's crowd eliminated. And we need LePaco eliminated."

"I'm confused," remarked Roller.

"Of course you are, you dumb bastard. What our bartending friend has told me changes everything. We use these two as bait to get LePaco here. We get his reward. We torture him so he tells us the location of the Four I's hub. We off him and then destroy whatever planet they're running their operation from."

"Then we go after that fancy artifact," interjected Noot.

"Yes. We might want to kill these two at some point before that," concluded Hefty.

"What if I could tell you where the Four I's main hub is located?" said Duke.

Hefty Senchax's eyes darted to the Nova Texan.

"Can you?" slurped the husky criminal.

"If you take executing us off the negotiation table."

CHAPTER 4

YOU STUPID ORB

"IT'S JUST NOT GOING TO happen. Not in a million cycles. With all due respect, of course."

Hefty Senchax pondered Duke's statement for a moment. A few gaseous belches exited the gang boss' mouth. The stench was so putrid that Duke could actually feel the odor stick against his skin.

"And why, pray tell, won't LePaco come down here in person?" asked Hefty. "I'm not some ordinary thug running a two-bit operation on a backwoods planet in a backwoods system, LaGrange."

"Of course not, your worthiness," Duke replied with a bow. "That never crossed my mind and it has nothing to do with anything. He wouldn't come down in person for anyone, especially Ish and me. We just aren't that important, reward notwithstanding."

"You know, the more I think of it," Senchax began, "it wasn't *that* big of a reward."

Should I be offended? thought Duke. "He'll just send some Four I's lackeys to verify it's us and that'll be the end of it. You'll be wired the credits—or he'll turn his ships on you and the rest of Prime."

"He wouldn't dare," gasped the crime lord.

"He would. The Four I's goal is to control the entire universe and, though some might argue the value of Prime's role within the universe, it still is part of it. The Four I's will get here eventually. It might as well be when they take us in. It's the most efficient... and they love efficiency."

"Garbage!" Senchax blurted. "Utter nonsense! They wouldn't dare attack Prime."

"I hate disagreeing with someone as wise and well-thought of..." Duke began.

He was cut off by Senchax. "Stop with the empty praise already, LaGrange! LePaco is smart; he knows not to attack us."

"Oh exalted one..."

"LaGrange!"

"I'm sorry, Mr. Senchax, but he will. They will. It's only a matter of time."

The obese crime lord didn't respond immediately. Once again, he appeared to be in deep thought, analyzing the bounty hunter's line of thinking. It was such deep thought that he allowed two different servants to pass by with trays full of sweets and other delicacies without taking so much as a sniff.

"What do you think?" asked Hefty.

The Booze Man re-emerged from his shadowy corner behind the gang boss.

"It's an interesting choice that has to be made. Use these two as bait and hope that LePaco either comes and we can kill him, or that he sends his goons and the reward, but has no intentions of an attack on Prime. If we do this, we give ourselves more than one outcome that could be considered a win."

"Yes, yes," Senchax blurted, "I knew we should stick to our original plan. They won't attack us."

"But," the Booze Man interjected.

"Oh. What?" Hefty replied dejectedly, as if he knew the Booze Man's next words.

"If this Nova Texan and his friend really do know where the Four I's headquarters is, and if we can destroy it... that would eliminate the biggest threat to your enterprises and render LePaco useless."

Except for the universe-altering mega-weapon he's trying to assemble, Duke thought to himself.

"So you outlined the choices—now what do *you* think I should do?" snapped Senchax.

The Booze Man approached and knelt down before his boss. Duke couldn't hear the conversation, but he didn't have to wait long to learn the Booze Man's recommendation.

"You're a lucky man, LaGrange," began Senchax. "A *really* lucky man."

Noot and Roller both stomped their feet and sighed. It was clear that they wanted to see pain inflicted on their prisoners.

"My colleague seems to think that we should give you a chance to earn your freedom."

"Why thank you, your grace," Duke said, bowing again. "I'm sorry, I mean Mr. Senchax. You won't regret this. I have some ideas on how to take the Four I's out; I've fought them before. Their fleet is impressive. They've constructed a few Armada Titans, dozens of battle cruisers, hundreds of scouts —" He stopped mid-thought. "What type of operation, arms-wise, are we sending out?"

Hefty chuckled to himself.

The Booze Man walked in front of his employer. "Not enough to win a straight-on dogfight, if their fleet is as impressive as you state. We'll signal the top bosses on Prime and in the sector. I'm not sure how many will trust us that this is legit. And for the ones that do come, I'm not sure how many *we* can trust."

"Great."

"Even with a better-than-expected turnout, we will still be

overmatched from a numbers standpoint. We will have to use other tactics to get the job done. We have the element of surprise on our side."

"Unless LePaco's already infiltrated some of the other syndicates," Duke countered.

"True. A risk we have no way of avoiding."

"So, best case, how many ships do you think we have?"

The Booze Man looked back at Hefty. The boss shrugged his shoulders, jiggling the rolls of neck that rested on them.

"We have a dozen or so that are battle-ready, including Mr. Senchax's flagship. It won't take down an Armada Titan but it'll leave a few scars to remember us by."

"A dozen? Maybe we should revisit this 'me as bait' plan."

"If some of the other bosses agree, we can probably field a few hundred more."

Still probably outnumbered twenty-to-one and outgunned a thousand-to-one, thought Duke. *Why did I recommend this plan again?*

"The *Deus* packs a punch too."

"The what?" asked Hefty.

"My ship."

"You think I'm going to let you fly your own ship?"

"We need all the firepower that we can get if we're going to—"

"LaGrange, are you an idiot? You think I'm just going to trust you to stand with us—the people that wanted to kill you a few minutes ago—and fight a seemingly insurmountable battle against the Four I's, when you could easily turn your ship around and escape?"

"Kinda. Yeah. We *need* the *Deus*."

"Your ship stays here. You'll be on the flagship. If the base isn't where you say it is, well, let's just say that you'll be hoping that we forked you over to LePaco."

"And if we win, I can trust you to just bring me back to Prime and let me go?"

"The Four I's will be destroyed in that scenario, correct?" asked the Booze Man.

"Yes," answered Duke.

"LePaco will know that we did it, so his readiness to deal with us is going to be null and void."

"You make a good point there."

"So what value will you have to Mr. Senchax?"

Duke didn't want to say it but he knew it was true. His ego would be bruised yet again.

"None."

"That's right, none!" shouted Hefty from behind the bartender. His belly laugh did the size of his belly justice.

Ishiro'shea tugged at Duke's arm. He held up three fingers.

"Three what?" inquired Duke.

The ninja repeated the motion.

"I have no idea what you are talking about?"

Ishiro'shea then took his hand and pointed to the middle of his forehead. He repeated this motion over and over again.

"That's right!" screamed Duke euphorically. "Mr. Senchax, I might have a way to level the playing field a bit. Now, it might not sound logical at first, but it could be just what we need."

"And that is?" asked the crime boss. The Booze Man squinted skeptically.

"I know a group that might help us."

"How much do they cost?" asked Senchax.

"Nothing."

The gang boss' attention perked up.

"They are just as interested in seeing the Four I's removed from the universe. In fact, I've seen them, firsthand, take out an Armada Titan."

"It would take an entire fleet to do that," noted the Booze Man.

"An entire union," replied Duke with a huge smile.

"A union?" asked the bartender.

"The Bounty Hunters Union."

The crime lord's earlier belly laugh was dwarfed by his response to this proclamation. His laughter caused his body to quiver and gyrate until Duke thought his sofa throne might snap.

"You think that exists? It's a legend; a story that criminal mommies tell their delinquent offspring to get them to practice their money laundering exercises. It's not real. LaGrange, you are an idiot."

Duke's fists clenched.

The Booze Man walked back again to advise Senchax. There was a long, drawn-out silence. It was so quiet that Duke could hear Noot and Roller mouth-breathing heavily behind him.

Hefty readjusted himself, wiping away from his top chin rolls pools of saliva that had escaped his mouth during his fit of hilarity.

"Duke," he said with a bit more composure, "even if these mysterious union members did exist, I have no interest in dealing with bounty hunters. Do you realize how much I would be worth to them?"

"I do, actually. And it pales in comparison to what it's worth to destroy the Four I's. They're trying to outlaw bounty hunting."

"The only thing that I agree with them on," replied Hefty.

"They could really help us. At least let me arrange a meeting with Mama Fong."

"Mama Fong? That three-eyed Zylantian hussy! How's she still alive? Every crime boss worth his weight in credits has a hit out on her."

"Just talk to her. If a deal can be reached, then we have a much better chance of taking these guys out."

Hefty looked at the Booze Man, who nodded slightly to his rotund employer. "Fine, fine, fine. What can a quick chat hurt? And you can set this up?"

"Yes, absolutely. Immediately, in fact," replied the Nova Texan.

"Go ahead."

"Thank you, oh most opportunistic one," said Duke with an exaggerated bow.

"What did I say about the groveling, LaGrange?"

"My apologies."

"And of course, Duke will lead this one," commanded Hefty.

"Why thank you, Mr. Senchax," replied Duke. "I'm a little shocked but most honored to receive this newfound trust."

Hefty laughed again, finishing off a triumvirate of belly laughs that would register as small earthquakes on most planets.

"Oh not you, LaGrange. *This* Duke. Duke Dallas."

The Booze Man stepped in front of the gang boss and smirked at the two bounty hunters.

"I just realized that you both have the same first name," Hefty chuckled.

The elder Duke nodded.

"Aren't you from Nova Texas, too? Small universe," belched the gang boss.

Ishiro'shea and Duke LaGrange locked eyes. It was clear both were thinking the exact same thing.

Wrong father, you stupid Orb. Wrong flippin' father.

CHAPTER 5

SHOCKINGLY SOUND

THE SLIDING DOORS OPENED. LIGHT from the control center that served as the operational nervous system of Hefty Senchax's entire enterprise transformed the dim corridor into something resembling a disco on acid. Duke Dallas, followed by T'ckuvian thugs Noot and Roller, exited with massive grins on their faces. Dallas tipped his Stetson to the younger Duke and Ishiro'shea. The Nova Texan wasn't sure what he thought about Dallas sporting a similar piece of headgear.

"Thanks, LaGrange," he smirked. "Your friend is a shrewd businesswoman."

"So I'm guessing that something was worked out, Booze Man," LaGrange replied with no shortage of snark.

The bartender halted. Noot did too, but Roller wasn't as quick on the uptake and slammed into his partner. The T'ckuvians stumbled toward Dallas but he sidestepped the pair and they crashed into the floor. The two natives guarding Duke and Ishiro'shea helped the bumbling brutes back to their feet.

"Yes. Something was worked out," answered the Booze Man.

"Great."

"But I do think Fong wants a word with you alone."

"Oh, she does?" Duke said with an eye roll.

"What's your deal, LaGrange? I feel like there's something you want to say to me. And if you ask me, the only thing that you *should* be saying to me is 'thank you.' Senchax would've had your head."

"And it would have been the end of all of us. I don't need to thank you for coming to a logical conclusion and doing what's best for everyone, including your own skin."

Duke Dallas shrugged his shoulders as if to admit defeat. He tipped his hat again.

"Well, good luck with your chat regardless."

The Nova Texan didn't return the gesture. He and Ishiro'shea just headed directly into the control center and the awaiting leader of the Bounty Hunters Union.

"She did say alone," remarked Dallas.

"I know," replied Duke LaGrange.

"I'm just relaying what she said. No need to—"

"No, I mean *I know*." The Nova Texan stopped short of the threshold of the control center and turned to face the aging bartender. "I know who you are. I know who you are in relation to me."

There was a long, overly dramatic verbal standstill. Noot and Roller looked confused. The other guards looked disinterested. Duke Dallas looked as if he was trying to articulate his next comment but was coming up empty about how best to proceed.

"Wait, I should explain."

Probably should have thought a bit longer, concluded LaGrange.

Duke LaGrange turned around. The control center door slid shut, cutting off the four T'ckuvians and Dallas from him and Ishiro'shea.

The walls of the control center were covered in screens of various sizes. Some of the screens were broadcasting what appeared to be security feeds, others appeared to be showing dealings across a wide variety of business associates. There had to be over a hundred screens in the confined control room. Along the perimeter, two parallel rows of desks contained beings from a dozen different systems. They all faced the screens and appeared to be doing their part to keep Hefty's lucrative criminal enterprise afloat.

A subtle tug on his hand diverted Duke's attention to a diminutive alien known as a Broan.

"This way, Mr. LaGrange," he moaned. He was clearly not an enthusiastic little fella.

"We saw you earlier. At the Booze Man's joint."

"His prices are pretty reasonable," replied the Broan in the deadpan cadence typical of his species. "And there's not a lot of small talk. I hate small talk."

"Yeah, I bet," said Duke, sharing a glance with Ishiro'shea.

The trio stepped into a plastic booth. The Broan handed them each a minute earpiece. "See that screen straight ahead of you?"

"Yeah, the big one?"

"Yeah, the big one. That's where I'll broadcast your Zylantian friend. She's pretty aggressive, if you ask me."

"Thank you." Duke paused. "I don't believe I got your name?"

"Fogerly Crasstop."

"Thank you, Fogerly Crasstop."

The Broan closed the door to the cylindrical booth, walked to a panel and tapped away at a few buttons.

Mama Fong's face appeared on the primary screen. Her three eyes focused on Duke.

"It's an honor to talk to you again, Mama Fong."

"And you as well," she reciprocated. Given her manners, Duke had trouble understanding how Mama Fong grew up on such a disgustingly crude planet as Zylantia. "And, I must say, your friend Mr. Dallas, is quite the specimen."

Is she blushing? Is Mama Fong, the grizzled leader of the Bounty Hunters Union, actually blushing?

"I'm not following you?"

"Where have you been hiding him?"

"I just met him, Mama Fong."

"Oh, that's right. I apologize. He's just so charming. And easy on the eyes. That's saying a lot, LaGrange, since I have three. I think I might be a tad out of sorts. It's been a while."

Unbelievable.

"He's apparently a pretty significant part of Hefty Senchax's criminal empire," Duke reminded the Zylantian.

"I have no doubts about that. You know, Duke, if you really think about it..."

"Yes?"

"He's a bit like you."

That's because he's my deadbeat coward of a father that was too full of himself to finish raising an orphaned kid left to die in the heat of the Nova Texan sun.

"I hadn't noticed."

"He's like a slightly more rugged version of you."

Okay, there's that Zylantian congeniality.

"A similar energy, though." She took a breath, gathering herself. "But what do you think? Charm aside, what do you think of this alliance? Is it a trap?"

Duke knew that this potential alliance and his knowledge of the location of the Four I's headquarters were the two things keeping him alive. It was in his best interest to bet on the partnership being on the up-and-up, because anything else would likely find him on the down-and-down. And if he didn't have the partnership, then attacking the Four I's was less of a strategic offensive and more of a suicide mission. The truth was, he wanted to believe Duke Dallas' intentions. He wanted to believe that Hefty Senchax, despite building a multi-planetary empire by double-crossing every person he came across, was capable of seeing that this was the most logical way to take out the oppressive Four I's contingent. He really, really wanted to.

"I don't think it's a trap, no."

"But?" Mama Fong asked.

"I do think that Hefty and any of the crime bosses that decide to join will be quick to turn once the outlook grows the slightest shade of grim."

"Honor amongst thieves?"

"Not with this lot. They give thieves a bad name. A more financially prosperous name, but a bad one, nonetheless."

"I see."

"Even so, I do believe that Senchax and his operation are aligned to the fact that a joint attack with the BHU is the best, most plausible way to take out the Four I's. After that, I wouldn't even try and guess his intentions."

"Do you believe this Dallas character?"

"Why does that matter?" Duke snapped.

Mama Fong squinted with all three eyes.

"I'm sorry," the bounty hunter recoiled. "I'm a bit jumpy. It's hasn't been a smooth trip here to Prime."

"Understood, LaGrange."

"Yeah, I believe him. As much as anyone, I guess. What were the terms of the partnership anyways?"

"Pretty standard. We coordinate together as equals. If we can't land on a joint plan, then we don't pursue further. However, assuming that we align on a strategy that both parties feel can win, we do our best to have our teams operate independently."

"I could see how bounty hunters ordering gang bosses around, or vice versa, could be interesting."

"And not productive."

"And if we're successful?"

"We agreed to give them a grace period."

"For what?"

"A grace period of one cycle that we won't pursue those

that aided in the battle. In fact, Dallas seemed to think it would be a fairly significant recruiting tool."

"Is that wise?"

"Financially speaking, we will survive. They will be paying us a portion of the fair market value of the bounties on their respective heads. It will be placed into a third party account and distributed over time in equal increments until the cycle has ended."

"Shockingly sound."

"I was surprised too. That Dallas character knows his stuff."

Except how to be a decent father.

"Agreed on plan... Grace period... A fair market fee to leave them alone. Seems pretty airtight."

"Dallas did have one more request."

"What's that?"

The Zylantian's mouth puckered. "He demanded that you remain with him under Hefty's control, at least until the assault is over."

"And?"

"And what? That's why I wanted to talk to you. You're one of the longest-standing members in our ranks. You've never missed a single BHU payment. I won't agree to this without your blessing. Our union is only as strong as our members."

For the first time in what felt like a dozen cycles a warm feeling consumed Duke's body. There was no life-long love selling him out to Admiral LePaco. There was no intergalactic dogfight with an Armada Titan. There was no kidnapped child or swarm of swamp people or power gauntlets. He felt *happy*. Duke searched his memory to remember the last time that he truly felt this way. It was his last night on Neprius. A night with a beautiful, powerful lady.

"Mama Fong, thank you. But it would be selfish—even for me—to deny a chance to take out the Four I's and, possibly,

LePaco because of my imprisonment. I'm fine going along with the plan."

Ishiro'shea stepped in front of Duke.

"Ish, you can't go instead of me. I got this."

The ninja pointed to himself adamantly.

"No, you can't join me either. Maybe we can negotiate with Hefty to get the *Deus* back and you can join the BHU fleet."

Ishiro did not yield.

"Guys," Mama Fong interjected, "I think Hefty meant both of you."

Duke noticed Ishiro'shea smiling under his mask.

"I'm not sure when I will be in contact with you again but, on behalf of your brothers and sisters in the Bounty Hunters Union, good luck. Good luck to both of you. I hope we meet again soon."

"In a world without Admiral LePaco and the Four I's."

"That's the plan," Fong replied.

The screen went black. A sharp ringing stung Duke's ears.

"Holy hedgehogs!" Duke screamed.

The ringing smoothed to become the monotone voice of Fogerly Crasstop.

"Sorry about that. But you have another communication coming in," muttered the Broan.

"From who?"

"The boss."

Hefty Senchax appeared on the large screen. His bulbous face extended well beyond the monitor.

"I just talked to Dallas," said the crime lord in between belches that didn't quite escape his mouth, "and it looks like you came through. We might have a chance to take out those bastards after all."

"Looks like," said Duke.

"We start our planning tomorrow with your bounty hunter

friends. But tonight we celebrate. I want you and Ishiro'shea to be our honored guests."

"We are definitely honored, Mr. Senchax."

Duke turned to Ishiro'shea and whispered, "I've heard how nuts his parties are; this alone could be worth all that we've been through on this dump of a planet."

"Excellent," said Hefty. "It's going to be one of the biggest events that I've ever thrown, even at this short notice. Many of the other gang bosses are attending. It's going to be epic."

"Sounds fun."

"I even scored the biggest cover band in the sector."

"Congratulations, I'm sure they will add to the marvel of the spectacle."

"The Stampeding Lifeless Androids. You know who they cover?"

"I have an idea, Mr. Senchax."

CHAPTER 6

A CHAT

HEFTY'S FLAGSHIP WAS IMPRESSIVE. IT was larger than one of the Four I's battle cruisers and appeared to pack as much firepower as an Armada Titan. Clearly, Senchax's bottomless pockets had allowed him to build an intimidating lead vessel. The other gang bosses had impressive ships as well, but Hefty's was something different. Of course, Hefty wasn't *on* the ship. He wasn't about to actually risk his own neck. It was probably a smart decision: Duke assumed that his father was probably more adept in combat than the obese crime lord.

Duke and Ishiro'shea sat on the bridge without any constraints.

Who knew a criminal enterprise could be so trusting? thought Duke.

The bridge was cavernous and followed a similar design to the control center. Screens filled every open space and a litany of races filled the seats, all staring at those screens. Hefty employed the best, regardless of their planet of origin.

The main doors on the back wall slid open. Duke Dallas, trailed by Noot and Roller, stepped over the threshold. The crew all paused and acknowledged the senior officer on the deck with a diverse round of salutes, nods, grunts, and head-shakes. Ishiro'shea even extended a thumbs-up.

"Put that down, Ish. He's not *our* captain," said Duke.

"More like cap*tor*," interjected Dallas.

Duke struggled to think of a retort.

"No need for a witty comeback, Duke. I wasn't being serious. You and Ishiro'shea are free men on my ship."

"You are too kind, my liege," Duke replied with a mocking bow. "You are too generous for scum like us."

Duke Dallas sat down in a chair next to the two bounty hunters. He sported a cheerful expression.

"We missed you at Hefty's gala. I hope you're feeling better."

"Much better. Must have been food poisoning," Duke replied.

"You didn't miss much. I wasn't a huge fan of the musical act. I guess I'm not a fan of their source material."

"Yeah, I hear they aren't for everyone," Duke responded, exchanging a quick glance with Ishiro'shea.

A Sabromm approached and handed Duke Dallas a device. He input a few lines of data and handed it back to the thick-skulled crewman. "Thanks, Jerry."

"You're welcome, Captain."

Duke Dallas turned back to the bounty hunters.

"Tardasio System, huh? I should've guessed that. Makes sense. We know the Tardasians aren't going to put up much of a resistance. They're isolated. They have plenty of uninhabited moons and planetoids to set up a nifty little operation."

"Yep, Tardasio," Duke replied, uninterested in the conversation.

"Did you hear about the plans? Surprisingly, the crime syndicates worked well with the BHU," stated Dallas.

"I think bounty hunters and criminal masterminds are probably closer in makeup than one might imagine."

"I don't doubt that," Dallas concurred. "It's a sound strategy. I think we have a chance."

"Possibly."

"And more folks joined up than anticipated. I think news of Oscavia and Erontia falling to the Four I's really hit home. I think they also are close to taking over the entire Ecclox System as well."

"Neat."

The Nova Texan stood up and turned his back on the elder Duke.

Dallas sighed deeply. "Look, I know I owe you a chat."

"You don't owe me anything," Duke snapped back. "As far as I'm concerned, when you left after Trixie was murdered, you were as dead as she was."

"That was a long time ago, Duke."

"I know, so long ago that it's like it never happened. In fact, maybe it didn't. I was young, after all. Maybe it was a figment of my imagination; something to fill the gap after Miss Trixie died. Yeah, I like that story better. I'm going to go with that."

"Duke, please. There *was* a reason."

"Nah, I think I'll stick to my story, if you don't mind."

Duke Dallas plunged his face into his hands. "Look, when Trix died, it hit me hard. The only thing I could think about was revenge. I had to see that son of a bitch mutilated and torn to bits and scattered across the cosmos. It consumed me. I couldn't be a parent. So I left. I had every intention of returning. I thought it would be a few weeks, tops. But the bastard proved to be harder to track. And I just couldn't give up. I knew the girls at Trixie's place would take good care of you."

"You do realize you left me to be raised in a brothel, right?"

"I didn't at the time. I mean, I knew it was a brothel but I didn't consider it 'leaving you.' I thought I'd be right back. But I didn't realize that I'd be so consumed by murderous intent. Death. Killing. But, hey, I couldn't have been all bad, right? You took my name."

The younger Duke shook his head. "First off, you gave me a dumbass name to begin with."

"What? Lafayette? Trix loved that name."

"The reason I was called Duke was only because one of the girls told me you died in battle and you were a hero. When I learned that wasn't the case, it was too late. Everyone knew me as Duke. I even tried to change it but it didn't stick."

"Change it to what?"

"I had a few phases. I went simple. Tom."

"You're not a Tom. You're a Lafayette. You're a Duke," replied Duke Dallas.

"Then I went with Hacksaw LaGrange."

"I'm guessing no luck there either?"

"Have you called me 'Hacksaw LaGrange' yet?"

"Touché."

"I even had a time when I just referred to myself as 'The Jaguar.'"

Duke Dallas did not respond.

"So don't flatter yourself that I go by Duke. It had nothing to do with you, or the real you, at least," said LaGrange.

"Fair enough."

"Did you at least track him down? Did you get your revenge?"

"It took a while."

"What's a while?"

"Fifteen cycles."

"Holy hedgehogs. I'll give you kudos on the dedication."

"I came back to Nova Texas a few times to check in on you. I was too embarrassed. The longer I stayed away and the older you got, the more embarrassed I felt."

"I'm glad a bout with embarrassment was too much to overcome. I know I wasn't your flesh and blood, but you should've told Mom that you weren't interested in a son if something happened to her. She could've made arrangements or sent me back to an orphanage."

"About that—" Dallas began.

"It was almost as bad as my real parents who dumped me on the doorstep of a brothel. Abandoning a kid a second time is pure evil."

He stormed away from Ishiro'shea and his adopted father. *Let's see if I really have freedom on this ship.*

The hall that led from the bridge to a centralized elevator bank was dotted with chairs, benches, and other furniture to accommodate the weary space traveler. Duke plopped down on a resting apparatus designed for a T'ckuvian. He closed his eyes and attempted to collect his thoughts.

After an undeterminable amount of time, he awoke. Sitting next to him was his Irish-Japanese companion.

"Hey, Ish."

The ninja greeted him silently.

"I'm sorry about that. I need to focus on getting out of here. And I hate that the *Deus* is back on Prime collecting dust. I miss her."

Ishiro'shea agreed again.

"I'm worried that this detour with the Four I's is going to put us behind on our real mission. Even if we take out the Four I's, it doesn't matter if LePaco finds your parents and the Amplification Key."

The ninja placed his hand on Duke's shoulder.

"I hope you're right, Ish. I hope it will all work out. I'm just not so sure with that bastard running the ship. Let's just hope he's a better captain than he was a father. Can you believe that load of garbage he was shoveling at me?"

Ishiro'shea shrugged.

"No, don't tell me that you believed it," cried Duke. "C'mon, Ish."

"Lafayette LaGrange," shouted Duke Dallas.

"Where did you come from? I'm done with your apologies or whatever that was. No more. Let's just try and beat these guys and go on our merry ways."

"Lafayette LaGrange, you weren't adopted. Not by me, at least."

"Is this supposed to make me feel better? Or you?"

"Trixie wasn't your biological mother. But her last name *was* LaGrange."

"Yes, I know this. Should I go get your 'Father of the Year' trophy now?"

"We both decided to give you that name so that you weren't dishonored by your biological father. He was a nasty, nasty man that did a lot of nasty things. He was a bounty hunter, back when that wasn't a glamorous gig with unions and fanfare. It was a hard, gritty way of life. It wasn't pretty. It was a different time, especially on a place like Nova Texas."

"And this degenerate was?"

"It was me, you ass. *You* are my flesh and blood. I cared for you, alone, when you were an infant. When I met Trixie, she fell in love with you, as she and I fell in love. We were a family. But knowing my occupation and reputation, I didn't want anyone to know that you were my son. You would've been a target. It was Trixie's idea for us to make up the story that you were orphaned and she adopted you. We thought it would give you a fighting chance to survive."

"So my last name is actually 'Dallas'?"

"Yes."

Duke scratched his chin as he tried to ignore the bowling ball being manufactured in his stomach. "I'm going to stick with LaGrange, if that's okay with you."

"I think that's fair."

"And who's my real mother, then? Who abandoned me at birth to be reared by a notorious, deadbeat bounty hunter with the parenting skills of a soggy hush puppy?"

"That's a different story for a different time, Duke."

Duke stood up and stretched. He was still trying his best to appear unfazed by the news. It was a battle that he knew he couldn't win in the long term.

"Look, I know this is a lot to process," Duke Dallas began. "But I wanted to tell you just in case this is the last time that we see each other."

A T'ckuvian, a Broan, and a Sabromm sprinted down the hall and placed themselves between the father and son.

"Sir," began the Sabromm.

"Yes, Jerry."

"We're at the rendezvous point. The other crime lords are wanting to know when we start the attack on Tardasio."

The elder Duke turned to his son. "I'm sorry that everything turned out how it did. I'm sorry—"

"Sir, we need to go," insisted Jerry.

Duke Dallas turned back and headed towards the bridge.

"Dallas," the younger Duke shouted.

"Yes?"

"Sorry about the 'Father of the Year' jab."

CHAPTER 7

AN UNDENIABLE RIGHT

THE PLAN WAS SIMPLE ENOUGH. The bounty hunters would blitz Tardasio 5 with the full strength of their force, hoping to catch the Four I's napping. The expected retaliation would lead to a pitched space battle and, assuming that the BHU could properly feign retreat to draw the Four I's away from their home facility, it would leave the main operations relatively unguarded. At this point, the tenuous allegiance of crime lords, gang bosses, and all-round bad hombres would emerge from the shadows of the uninhabited Tardasio 2 and launch a full-scale assault on the weakened hub of the Four I's. The battle would need to be swift because, as impressive as the BHU-crime lord tandem was, the Four I's could easily send reinforcements from neighboring systems and create a one-sided affair. With the arms manufacturing facility down and a major blow to the Four I's central command achieved, the conquered planets would be able to fight back without having to worry about an endless stream of battle cruisers and soldiers sent to squash any rebellions.

Duke knew the plan could work, barring any creative ideas from the criminal element of the team. He also knew that it would all amount to nothing if Admiral LePaco retrieved the

Amplification Key. Unfortunately, at the present, Duke and Ishiro'shea were stationed on Hefty Senchax's lead battleship at the vanguard of an impending invasion.

All of the crewmen on the bridge were focused on the task at hand. Duke Dallas wasn't sitting in the captain's chair, nor was he even in the captain's area. He moved from crew member to crew member, reviewing every last detail of the strategy.

He locked eyes with his son. He smiled. "Glad you two decided to join us up here for the push."

Duke didn't respond. Ishiro'shea bowed slightly.

"I'm just making sure our preparations are airtight," Dallas began. "I'm not really a 'figure it out as I go' type of guy."

Ishiro'shea chuckled. Duke smirked at his co-conspirator.

"I can make plans and triple-check 'em if I want to," Duke whispered to Ishiro. It was met with an exaggerated eye roll.

"What was that, Duke?" asked Dallas.

"Nothing. Never mind. What's the ETA on the attack?" Duke asked in an attempt to change the subject.

"We're just waiting for the word from Mama Fong. Once she feels that they've pulled the main force away from the planet, we're up."

"And you feel like you can trust these guys?" Duke gestured at the forward screen. "I'm sure Glortos 'Iron Jaw' Reebor isn't super comfortable working with Hefty. Or the Great Poison King of Hyptox, Flaph Goomshoot. Or the Cyclopsian Syndicate. Or—who is that out there? Is that the Gang of the Mystic Saber? How can you trust those nutjobs?"

Duke Dallas laughed.

"I don't trust them at all. But I trust that they understand what would happen to each of us if the Four I's and Admiral LePaco are allowed to continue doing what they're doing. I don't see an alternative."

You have no idea what LePaco is doing, old man, thought Duke. He bit his tongue.

"And they all signed off on their assignments. The Cyclopsian Syndicate is going to hit the facilities in the Southern Hemisphere. With their fleet and the relative size of the planet, that should be easy for them."

"They like blowing things up," noted Duke.

"Yes, they do."

"Goomshoot and Reebor are focusing on the major plant at the northern pole. It's heavily guarded—too much for one squad, I believe. I figured they have the best chance of working together seeing as they're related."

"And the Sabers?"

"Since they have the greatest number of ships in their fleet, they're going to join the BHU and cut off the Four I's from behind."

"And, let me guess, you'll be leading the run on the Four I's headquarters outside of Pentos City?"

"Yes. With the weapons in our fleet, we have the best chance of crippling it."

"Good plan. Pretty basic. But good," concluded Duke.

Before Dallas could respond, Mama Fong's face filled the screen adjacent to the forward view. Her three eyes were sparkling. "Great news, Dallas. The Four I's took the bait. They sent their entire force out to take us down."

"Are you outnumbered?"

"Oh, considerably," Fong replied, with no less enthusiasm.

I've never seen someone so happy about being overmatched in battle, thought Duke.

"But they're leaving the planet?" asked Dallas.

"In droves. Hold, please." Fong cut communication.

The bridge remained silent as they awaited her return.

Fong's face reappeared. "Sorry, I had a few on my tail. Anyways, the news of us taking down the Armada Titan must've reached Tardasio 5, because they sent the entire cavalry. Right now, it's some battle cruisers and a few random craft that I haven't seen before."

"No Titans?" blurted Duke.

The entire crew turned to look at him. Each being flashed what constituted a scowl or grimace, depending on their physiology.

"Oh, nice to see you again, LaGrange," said Mama Fong. "No, no Titans yet. I thought we'd see a few guarding the planet. But I'm not going to look a gift narwhal in the mouth."

"So are we clear to go?" interjected Duke Dallas anxiously.

"All clear," replied the Zylantian bounty hunter. "And good luck, Duke Dallas. I hope that our union proves beneficial and worthwhile."

"You and me both, Mama."

The Zylantian cut communication.

Duke Dallas turned his back on the view screen image of Tardasio 2. "It's time, everyone. I know you've each made a good living working under Mr. Senchax. And I also know that this mission falls well outside of your ordinary duties for Hefty, excepting those that he hired specifically for this mission. We wouldn't be asking this of you if it wasn't vital to the future of the business. I also thank you for your trust in me to lead this battle. It will get hairy. Dicey. Messy. It might even appear that the desired outcome can, in no way, happen. But even in the bleakest of moments, stick to the game plan. Follow me. Follow our strategy and we will knock these sons of bitches on their asses."

The bridge erupted. Duke turned to see a gleeful Ishiro'shea giving Duke Dallas a thumbs-up.

"For Hefty!"

The bridge returned the chant. Noot and Roller let loose primal screams of excitement.

Sheep, Duke thought. *Nothing but a bunch of sheep.*

Duke Dallas composed himself and began to issue directions. "Jerry, put the others on the screens."

"Everyone, sir?"

"Yes."

The other criminal kingpins appeared on screens of various sizes. They were all there: the Great Poison King of Hyptox; Iron Jaw; the Illustrious Potentate of the Gang of the Mystic Saber; Professor Krob, Chief Executive Officer of the Cyclopsian Syndicate.

"We have the green light from the bounty hunters," Dallas began. "You each know your roles. When we talk again, let's hope it's in a universe in which we can still openly lie, cheat, steal, and blackmail—for that one, undeniable right that should be afforded to all beings..."

Each crime boss leaned in a little closer to the screen, eagerly awaiting the conclusion of Dallas' speech.

"...to get filthy rich," Dallas finished.

This was the solitary connective tissue that held the motley bunch of scum together. Duke Dallas knew that. His son suspected that the crime bosses would follow the plan as it was laid out... as long as it didn't seem like the Four I's were going to win.

CHAPTER 8

THE NORTH POLE

THE CYLINDRICAL VESSEL HOVERED ABOVE the southern continent of Tardasio 5. It looked like nothing more than a floating iron log, drifting in space, as nondescript as an intergalactic spaceship could be. Even the attack squadrons that surrounded it were boring—just miniaturized carbon copies of their prime. But what the vessel lacked in design aesthetics, it made up for in potency—militarily speaking.

The Cyclopsian Syndicate's bombing run was efficient and effective, much like their criminal enterprise. The smaller attack craft laid waste to the few tactical targets—a low-orbit cannon, a few missile stations that housed warheads that could likely reach them, a bit of this and that. Then the main ship let loose a bombing fury like no other. In a flash, the facilities in the southern half of Tardasio 5 were wiped from the face of the planet. Total obliteration. There would be no more ship and weapon construction there.

"The Professor's hailing," screamed Jerry, the Sabromm officer. "I'm putting him through."

The leader of the Cyclopsian Syndicate, Professor Claudius Krob, appeared on the primary screen. His appearance was in total contrast to Hefty Senchax and most other crime lords; he was well-groomed, for starters. His hair was pristine, his teeth a sparkling white, and he sported a specially-designed monocle with temples to simulate an ordinary pair of two-eyed reading glasses.

"The mission has been completed," said the Professor in a soft but commanding tone. Duke noted subtle tones of happiness and appreciation in the Cyclopsian's voice. It was very odd.

"Yes, it appears so," answered Dallas. "We were able to witness most of it. Quite impressive."

"Thank you. It was our pleasure to help in this endeavor. We will now proceed to phase two of our responsibilities and assist the Mystic Saber in their efforts. Please pass along my well-wishes to our brothers, Glortos and Flaph, as they attempt to isolate the forces in the North."

"I'll do that, Professor," replied Dallas.

The transmission ended.

Duke LaGrange and Ishiro'shea sat along the back wall of the bridge.

"You know, Ish, if this raid goes sideways, we're stuck up here. We're going down with this thing."

The ninja nodded.

"I never pictured us going out at as prisoners on a criminal's ship, captained by my biological father, during an attack run on some well-organized middle-management types."

It was clear that the ninja agreed with this statement even more.

"Jerry, patch me through to Reebor and Goomshoot," ordered Duke Dallas.

"Together or individually?"

"Together is fine."

The Sabromm plugged away. Within moments two faces appeared on the screen. Two faces that, despite being related in some form or fashion, looked nothing alike.

Glortos "Iron Jaw" Reebor was familiar to Duke. Before he started his criminal organization, the Glortos Reebor Experience, and was just a lowly thief, Duke and Ishiro'shea had almost brought him in on Oscavia. Unfortunately, Duke let his carnal proclivities cloud his focus, as had many before him on Oscavia, and the weaselly Reebor had slipped off the planet.

"I can't believe that pesky fleabag became so successful," Duke whispered to Ishiro'shea. "To think that we had him in our sights back in the caves."

The Irish-Japanese ninja just rolled his eyes.

"What? You can't hold that one against me. Anyone in my position, literally *that* position..." started Duke, but he trailed off as his memory of the event became clearer... and more graphic.

"What do you want, Dallas?" shrieked the pint-sized Reebor from the view screen. Though he lacked an imposing stature, his voice was amplified enough for him to be mistaken for the hardiest of species. In fact, his nickname of "Iron Jaw" originated from a tale that he took down a Mega-Troll by chomping down on his ankle and not letting go until the behemoth collapsed in exhaustion, pain, and probably a bit of embarrassment. As with many of Reebor's claims, there had been no witnesses.

"I don't have all day, ya' know," Reebor smirked.

"Nice to see you again, Glortos," Dallas responded. "And you, Flaph."

While it was hard for Duke to believe that Reebor had built up a successful organization in spite of his uninspiring physical appearance, it was even harder to believe that Flaph Goomshoot had built up an equally lucrative business in spite of his very limited mental resources. In fact, the menacing moniker that he advertised at every moment possible—the Great Poison King of Hyptox—was rumored to relate less to a strategic dealing of death to a rival and his entire planet of followers, and more to a bit a dumb luck involving a fortuitous missile guidance miscalculation and an unsuspecting ship carrying highly toxic chemicals away from Hyptox's decomposing moon. His Hyptoxian rivals were never heard from again. The event would go down in history as a shrewd tactical maneuver that was both clever and coldhearted. The ironic fact was that Goomshoot was really neither of those things. No one would ever mistake him for a genius and, in Duke's interactions with him and his people, he seemed to be a pretty nice guy.

"Hiya, Dallas. How's my buddy, Hefty? Still fat?" bellowed Flaph. He followed with a hearty laugh of throaty huffs and puffs. Goomshoot, unlike Glortos, was a behemoth. Bigger than a T'ckuvian, smaller than a Mega-Troll, and looked as if he was carved out of an iron boulder. Even with his colossal frame, his overall demeanor was as fluffy as a bunny dipped in fabric softener. Joke attempts notwithstanding.

"Yes, he's still struggling with his weight management," replied the captain. "I'll tell him that you asked after him."

"Oh, is that you, Glortos? How's my favorite relative?"

"Shut up, Flaph," jabbed Reebor. "The quicker Hefty's stooge gives us our directions, the quicker we can kill these bastards and get back to what's important."

"Family?" asked Goomshoot.

Iron Jaw planted his face deeply into his palm. He offered no response to his apparent family member.

"I can tell that you're both busy," interjected Dallas diplomatically, "and, to be honest, our mission has little room for error. So, I'll get right to it."

"Thank the gods," chimed in Reebor.

"Professor Krob checked in," said Dallas. "The Cyclopsian Syndicate succeeded in knocking out the southern camps. They're off to provide support for the Saber and the BHU. Now it's your turn. Remember the plan?"

"Yeah, yeah, yeah," screamed Reebor.

"Flaph?" asked Dallas.

"I think so. Yeah, no I got it. I remember."

"The pole is heavily guarded but it's their primary mining station for the ore they use to build their ships, including their Armada Titans."

The Nova Texan stood up from the back of the bridge. "And that ore is used as an additive to their fuel supply. We think that's how their craft can travel so far and so long without refueling."

The entire bridge crew looked back at LaGrange.

"What? It's true!" he shouted back.

"Wait a second," began Reebor. "Is that Duke LaGrange? The bounty hunter?"

"Yes, Glortos. It's me."

"You work for Hefty now? Now that's rich. I guess it makes sense."

"And why's that?"

"You were a pretty lousy bounty hunter."

Duke noticed a few giggles amongst the crew.

"You were lucky on Oscavia, pipsqueak. If that masseuse wasn't skilled in... Never mind. Anyways, I don't work for Hefty. It appears that he captured—"

"He's a special advisor for this mission," Dallas interjected. "He has some inside information on LePaco and the Four I's and accepted our generous offer to aid us."

"You're telling me that this mission was based on LaGrange's knowledge?" said Reebor with a groan. "Oh, we're as good as dead."

"Gnaw on any good ankles lately, Iron Jaw?"

"Stop it, both of you," commanded Dallas. He motioned for Duke to have a seat. "We're running out of time."

"Oh hey, Duke! Hey, Ishiro'shea! Nice to see you two again," chimed in Flaph, oblivious to the last few exchanges.

Duke waved back. Ishiro'shea extended a thumbs-up.

"Flaph, Glortos, are we good to go?" asked Dallas.

"Yeah," they both stated in tandem.

"Keep your visuals open. As soon as we see the mining facility damaged, we're heading in. Get out and join the rest."

"Got it," said Flaph. "When we're done, get some rest."

"No, you moron," barked Reebor, "he said 'join the rest,' got it?"

"Oh, I thought we were gonna blow up the Four I's facilities in the North," muttered the confused crime boss.

"Flaph," began Dallas, "you and Glortos go and blow those facilities at the northern pole to dust. When you're done, just follow Glortos."

"Got it."

Both men faded from the view screen.

Duke Dallas turned around to face his crew.

"Let's hope he knows where the North Pole is."

CHAPTER 9

A SHUT WINDOW

EXPLOSIONS DOTTED THE NORTHERN CONTINENT of Tardasio 5 like a bad case of acne. Flaph Goomshoot's flagship swung back over the fiery landmass and concentrated one last assault on the main mining facility. It was a direct hit. As his craft exited the lower atmosphere, the plant erupted in a giant blue fireball. A subsequent chain reaction was triggered by the salvo and, moments later, ancillary explosions burst from the mines themselves. Goomshoot and Reebor had successfully knocked out the entire operation in a matter of seconds.

"Good, good," Dallas muttered softly, only just audible enough for Duke to hear. "Now it's our turn."

He stood up and addressed all of his crew members again. *Clearly not his first time in front of a crew.* Stations were manned and attentions were focused on the pending attack.

"So not only is this main hub the most heavily guarded and not only is it situated beside the largest concentration of military outposts in the Tardasio System at Pentos City, but we are the final wave—which means they might actually be prepared for us," Duke said to Ishiro'shea. "Overall, it's a solid plan. Selfishly, I wish we would've been held captive on those Cyclopsian ships. Better life expectancy, I'm afraid."

"Are we ready, Jerry?" asked Duke Dallas.

The Sabromm officer nodded.

"Engage with mission protocol," commanded Dallas.

The imposing ship began to move. It had exited the shadows of Tardasio 2 and acquired a direct sightline to the Four I's planetary base before Duke could even blink.

This plan would really suck if the Tardasio System wasn't so densely packed, thought Duke.

"Forward, direct course to Pentos City. Patch me into our fighters, Jerry," commanded Dallas.

The Sabromm did as instructed.

"Team, Dallas here," he said, speaking into the communications panel, "you have your orders. Follow the course, don't veer off in the slightest. There'll be some anti-aircraft fire from Pentos City. They've had enough time to scramble a pretty salty defense. Ignore it and push through. We *have* to take down those facilities. I'll handle the forces in Pentos, then swing back and finish off the last of those plants... assuming y'all leave me any."

The pilots clearly relished Dallas' optimism. They all replied with a chorus of yips, yells, and sounds that could only be construed as a confident "Heck yeah, boss."

Duke walked over to Dallas. Jerry seemed annoyed that someone would approach the captain's chair without following proper protocol. But the Nova Texan didn't really care what the Sabromm thought.

"Hey, not to be a backseat pilot..." Duke began.

"But you're about to be one," Dallas replied.

"Yeah, kinda."

"Not right now, Duke. We're heading in. This is the proverbial 'it.' Too late for any revisions now."

"You're probably right," the bounty hunter responded. He

turned around and walked slowly to join Ishiro'shea at the back of the bridge.

"What is it?" Dallas huffed. "I know you have something to say, so just say it."

Duke spun around gleefully. "You agree that they've had enough time to request some backup, right?"

"Yes. They are nothing if not efficient."

"Right. But none have come through, right?"

"Correct. We have an entire squad guarding the nearest warp station. If they start to come through, we'll blast 'em before they know what hit 'em."

"Wonderful," said Duke. "And have they come through?"

"Nope. What are you getting at, Duke?"

"We're confident that they called for help. We're confident that help will come. We're confident that it hasn't come from the warp station. So..." Duke paused to allow Dallas to finish the thought.

"They're already here," Dallas replied, his tone suddenly solemn. "But we've scanned Tardasio 2. Tardasio 3 and 4 are accounted for as well. Tardasio 6 is so far away that an immediate strike isn't plausible."

"Same with Tardasio 1," added Jerry, obviously having eavesdropped on the conversation.

"The Tardasians aren't known for their facility with numbers," Duke replied.

"What does that even mean?" scowled Jerry.

"It means that—" Duke started.

Dallas cut him off. "Tardasio 7 is closer to us than Tardasio 6. Jerry, tell me we scanned Tardasio 7."

"We did not, sir," the Sabromm replied. "We didn't think that—"

"Full power ahead!" Dallas yelled. "Our window for success just shrank dramatically. We have to hit those targets before we *become* the targets."

"Full power!" echoed Jerry.

Hefty's flagship rattled and began its march towards Tardasio 5.

Then it rattled again—but this time it wasn't due to its engines. This rattling was from fire. Enemy fire. Fire from the ships that were hidden on Tardasio 7.

"Looks like our window might have just shut," Duke whispered to Ishiro'shea.

"Sir," started Jerry, "it might be worse than we feared."

"Go on," replied Dallas.

"They have an Armada Titan."

Murmurs permeated the bridge. Duke sensed the level of confidence dropping quickly. He could almost see it—like water gushing from a bucket with a brand new hole.

Dallas was calm. This was clearly not his first rodeo.

"Return fire. Protect the squadron at all costs. They have to destroy those targets."

The ship was rocked again.

The Titan.

"Hold steady. We have the best weapons in the gods-damn galaxy, let's use 'em!"

"They won't work on something that big!" replied a weapons officer.

"Then take out everything else. That ship can't take out all of our ships. Let them focus on us."

The command was met with some reluctance, though it seemed to Duke that they were following Dallas' orders. The ship was hit hard yet again but kept firing. Hefty had loaded it up with armaments that were neither legal on most planets nor even available in the general—or any—market. Rays and lasers and beams lit up the celestial battlefield. Some were obviously experimental but most proved effective against the Four I's lighter craft. The Titan showed no damage.

"Jerry, patch me in with Mama Fong. And the Saber."

"Done, sir."

Mama Fong, backed by a few other noted bounty hunters,

appeared on the screen first. Then at the bottom, an elderly humanoid popped up. His disheveled silver hair was in contrast to his weathered, burnt skin. He sported a conical hat of midnight blue, highlighted by accents the same color as his hair. He wore an eye patch.

"Have you ever seen one of the Mystic Sabers, Ish?" asked Duke.

Ishiro'shea shook his head. In fact, Duke didn't know anyone that had actually met one. They were a powerful criminal organization, but their work was subtle and discreet. They influenced more than coerced, and they were good at it.

"We have a problem," Dallas began. "There was a full reserve force on Tardasio 7. It's been activated."

"How big?" asked the Zylantian.

"Big enough. And they have an Armada Titan."

"I'm sorry, Dallas," Mama Fong continued, "we're in a scrap here. If we disengage, they're just going to follow us back to you."

"I know. How about the Saber?"

The man's expression did not change but his eyes closed. Then his head began to wobble slightly. After a few moments, his eyes opened.

"That's unfortunate," replied Dallas. "Make sure they don't get out of that warp station. Take out the station if you need to. There are other ways that *we* can get back."

He's a telepath, Duke realized. *No wonder the Saber and its members are so quiet.*

"If either of you can spare any support, we need it," Dallas pleaded. "Until then, we'll continue as planned." He cut the communication.

Another huge explosion on the outside of the ship forced a partial roll, throwing many of the officers from their stations. Duke Dallas held steady as if his feet were glued to the floor.

He looked over at Duke and Ishiro'shea. "You two, meet

me outside the bridge," he ordered. "Jerry, you're in control until I get back."

"What?"

"Jerry, it's not that hard. Just tell everyone to fire everything they've got. Protect our ships!"

"Yes, sir."

Duke and Ishiro'shea left the bridge. Dallas followed closely behind them.

"Over here," he said, motioning the bounty hunters into a nook in the hallway. The color was drained from his face; his cheeks hollowed. "Good call on the surprise attack, Duke. Very impressive."

"I kinda wish I'd been wrong on that one."

"I know. Look, you both know this isn't likely to end well," Dallas said, biting his lower lip.

"What? We can take 'em."

"No, Duke. I don't see a way that we survive this. I feel like it's my fault that you're here."

"No," began the Nova Texan.

"It is. Don't argue with me, please."

Okay, he's right, thought Duke. *It is.*

"So what do you need from us?"

"I have a feeling that there's more to the Heart of Nobunaga than you led us to believe. I don't know why. Call it fatherly intuition."

"Let's just call it plain ol' intuition for now," Duke remarked.

"Fine. But in my gut, it's part of all of this. About LePaco. The Four I's. Everything."

"And?"

Duke Dallas handed him an electronic card. "Take this."

"What is it?"

"I have a shuttle craft at the rear. It's not some escape pod; it's one of our attack ships, slightly modified. Fewer weapons but more speed. You and Ishiro'shea head back to T'ckuvu Prime and..."

"Wait. You're letting us bust out of this place?"

"Letting you? I'm giving you a map. Continue on your mission, whatever it is. Destroy LePaco."

"Thanks and all, but how are we going to get through the warp station? It's a war zone."

"This ship can get you far beyond this system, and quickly. I'm sure that you'll find an alternate route to Prime."

"And the card?"

"Go to Hefty's casino. Go to the parking garage and give this to the attendant. No need to say anything. Your ship will be there."

"He parked the *Deus* in his casino's parking garage?"

"Oh, and one more thing."

"Yeah?"

"Your weapons. I brought 'em. I stored them on the shuttle. I had a weird notion that you were going to have to use this craft."

More fatherly intuition? thought Duke.

The ship was hit hard again by the Four I's weaponry.

"Go! Now!" Dallas yelled.

"I don't know what to say. Thank you."

Duke Dallas grabbed his son's hand. He stared directly at him, his eyes unblinking.

"Seeing you again, even under these circumstances, has made me the happiest man in the universe. I now know what my son became—and it's exponentially better than anything that I could've imagined. Or that I deserve."

Dallas' eyes swelled. A steady trickle of tears fell down his cheeks and met his upturned lips. His smile subsided and became the terse expression of a leader facing a challenge that he couldn't win.

"Go, Duke LaGrange. Save the universe."

CHAPTER 10

THE LUCKIEST MAN ALIVE

VERY FEW CITIES ESCAPED THE global devastation of World War XVII, and during the hundred cycles since its conclusion, even fewer had managed to rebuild themselves. Kyoto was no different. The once burgeoning metropolis and cultural center of Japan had been reduced to ruins and subsequently abandoned by the survivors in the region. Generations came and went and Kyoto became just an area of dilapidated buildings beyond the mountains in the Yamashiro Basin. The people that sprung up around the deceased city chose to live a more simple lifestyle, feeding off the bounty of the land and the three rivers that called the basin home—the Ujigawa to the south, Kamogawa to the east, and the Katsuragawa to the west. This trio pumped life into the region from Lake Biwa to the northeast, one of the last bodies of water to remain uncorrupted by the war. The lake and its far-reaching tributaries were worshipped as deities.

"It's unusually cold today," said Ayuko Nobunaga as she dipped her finger into the steady current of the Katsuragawa. "I'm hoping that means the fish are extra eager to jump into my net."

"You've never had any problems with them before,"

replied Takeo. "I still think you trick them somehow. You're like a siren. The Fish Siren. You catch them like you caught me."

Ayuko blushed and splashed some water at her husband. "You're lucky to have me."

"I know, I know. And you're lucky to—"

"Yes? I'm lucky to what?" Lucky to have you?"

"I was going to say, lucky to live near such a beautiful city as Kyoto," Takeo said with a smirk. "Its beauty is only matched by yours, my sweet wife."

"Hey now," she pouted. "That's crossing the line, Takeo."

"You're right, my love. It's not funny to even kid about that smoldering heap of garbage that was once Kyoto."

"When I was a little girl, my grandfather told me about *his* grandfather telling him about it. It sounds like it was once a glorious place," said Ayuko. "Now, it's just a reminder of the war. I just wish the rivers could wash it out to Lake Biwa and we could start over. Build a new Kyoto."

"And the fact that those foreigners are still trying to find something there just makes it worse. The smoke and noise from their machines won't allow us to forget about it."

"What are they even looking for anyway?" asked Ayuko. "There's nothing there but mangled concrete and broken glass."

"I heard from the others in the village that the men are from Oceania—you know, the Coalition."

"Do they still run the world?"

"I think so," answered Takeo. "That's the beauty of being so isolated here—we don't have to worry about that. But the villagers told me that the Oceania Coalition men think there's a stash of active warheads buried below the city."

"From the Seventeenth World War?"

"I guess. Or the sixteenth. No, it's definitely the seventeenth."

"What was that one about again?"

"I don't remember, if I'm being honest. They all run together. I'm no history buff and I didn't really pay attention to Earth history in school."

"I bet it had something to do with those warheads. I doubt they're still active after all these cycles," said Ayuko.

"I don't know, they don't expire, do they? They could still be quite powerful. Maybe more powerful than anything they have now."

"Why do they need *more* powerful weapons? Or weapons at all? Has the planet recovered from the last war?"

"You're a dreamer, wife. A pretty dreamer but a dreamer, nonetheless. It has not recovered. And the recovery periods become longer after each war. Pretty soon, we won't ever recover. There will always be someone or some place that wants to control the rest. It's human nature."

The roar of a once-glorious skyscraper toppling over at the hands of the Oceania Coalition rumbled in the distance. The building must have been quite large as the seismic tremor rippled to the banks of the Katsugawara, sending Takeo into the shallow end rather unceremoniously. His wife giggled uncontrollably at the sight of her drenched husband.

"Hey, stop that! Or I'll throw you in here!" he joked.

"Then who would catch us dinner? I'm the only one that ever catches anything, remember?"

Still submerged in the water but now sitting up, Takeo wrestled with something in the folds of his shirt.

"Oh yeah? What do you call this then?" he asked. In his hands he clutched a wriggling Crucian carp.

"Luck."

"I call it dinner."

"Then *you* can cook it," Ayuko fired back, smiling.

Something else pressed against Takeo's chest. But it wasn't a fish. He reached into his shirt again but his smile turned to a confused frown.

"Did you catch breakfast for tomorrow as well, oh great fisherman of mine?"

"No... but I caught this." He pulled out a bright metallic pendant and showed it to his wife.

She shrugged her shoulders.

"Maybe I caught your birthday present?"

"I think the fact that you caught a fish is birthday present enough," she laughed.

Takeo examined the odd medallion. It looked weathered from countless cycles underwater, the current of the mighty Katsuragawa slowly breaking it down.

"I think it's ancient," he said. "It looks ancient. You know what? I'll apply it to the base my katana. It's not too heavy as to disrupt the balance of the blade."

"Great, junk on junk," said Ayuko, rolling her eyes.

"Antique on antique, you mean?"

"No, I meant junk. Just please don't let go of the—"

The carp squirmed out of Takeo's grasp and bolted down the river as if it had been shot out of a cannon.

"—fish," Ayuko finished.

"I'm sorry."

Ayuko glared at him. Her own fishing rod jolted and then bowed. She yanked on it, the fish bobbing on the river's surface in its fight to survive.

Takeo offered an innocent smile. "I really am the luckiest man alive."

Takeo Nobunaga and his family lived in a cozy wooden house raised above the ground. It was once the grain storehouse for the village, but when storage with double the capacity was erected, Takeo volunteered to move into the old one. The move to the storehouse allowed them to leave their previous and much smaller home to the community as a multipurpose facility. It hosted refugees. It held overflow from the school house. It was a dining hall. However, Takeo made sure to keep the back room off-limits to the public. This was his martial sanctuary. His *bugeikuden*. His dojo.

Not many Japanese adults practiced the martial arts anymore. With bombs and guns and missiles, there wasn't much need for a *gyaku nage* or a *haishu uchi* or a *kocho giri*. However, Takeo's father taught him the ways of a warrior, the ways of a *bujin*. His grandfather had taught his father in the same manner. Takeo's great-grandfather was a *kenshi*, a master swordsman, and his father was a real ninja. When he was alone in the dojo, be it practicing his strikes, meditating, or admiring his favorite possession—his family's katana blade— Takeo felt connected to his past and to his country.

Takeo was trying to perfect his *jiyu hakobuto* technique when his wife rapped on the outside wall of his dojo.

"Come quick, hurry!" Ayuko screamed.

"What's wrong?" Takeo opened the door to see his wife with her eyes wide with fear. "Calm down. What's wrong?"

"Men are here. With guns. They're in the middle of the village demanding to speak to someone in charge."

"There isn't anyone 'in charge.' Didn't someone tell them that?"

"Not exactly."

"What do you mean, 'not exactly'?"

"They all said that *you* were."

"What? Are they crazy? Why me?"

"Can you just come, please? If anyone can talk to them, it's you."

Takeo lowered his eyes and inhaled until he could feel his lungs expanding. He released a rush of air through his nostrils before he raised his head and locked eyes with his wife. "Did they say what they wanted?"

"No, just that they wanted to talk to the person in charge."

Ayuko yanked Takeo from his dojo and onto the stone

pathway that led from their old house and between two rows of housing. It was a short walk to the center of the village. In the distance Takeo could see flames from the visitors' torches rising above the straw rooves of the simple dwellings.

The husband and wife entered the circular field that marked the village's plaza, the gathering place for the locals. There were forty or fifty of Takeo's neighbors on one side; on the other were an equal number of foreigners, each decked out in camouflage fatigues. Each of them sported the OC insignia on their uniform or, as seemed to be the case with the grizzlier-looking members, tattooed on their biceps. Until now, Takeo's interactions with outsiders had been minimal, but, based on their skin color, he assumed most of them to be Australians or New Zealanders, the heart of the OC. Interspersed throughout the group were a few "Crazy Islanders," as they were referred to in Japan—known for their decorative tattoos that covered large swaths of real estate on their mahogany bodies. They were typically from Tonga or Samoa and were the muscle of the Coalition. No one messed with them and they were the primary reason that the OC had never lost a ground war.

Over time, the Coalition had conquered many of the other countries in the region, from Thailand to the Korean Peninsula. China had fallen to them thirty cycles ago. Japan, having been plunged into the deepest economic despair, was a Third World non-factor for many decades and avoided the ever-growing roster of Oceania Coalition countries. They didn't offer anything of value to the outside world until the discovery of a stash of potentially active warheads buried under Kyoto. Takeo noticed a pair of husky Mongolians flanking a fidgety Vietnamese soldier, the smallest man in the entire platoon. He was also the only one without an automatic weapon. He snarled and spit at the ground, all the while flashing two rusty knives.

Why is it that he's the one I'm most afraid of? Takeo wondered.

"This is the person in charge of our village," yelled one of the townsfolk. "Talk to him."

A man dressed from head to toe in solid khaki emerged from the gathering of soldiers. He was extremely wiry for such a short figure; his relatively long arms and legs seemed to explode from a truncated torso. His hands and feet were comically large for his frame; his face was long to the point where it was snout-like. Atop a ruddy brown mane sat a slouch hat with the words "Death Wallaby" inscribed across the front.

"My name's Aloysius Kelly. Ya' know me?" he sneered. "Of course ya' do. Everyone knows the Death Wallaby."

Should I tell him I have no idea who he is? Takeo asked himself.

"And who are you? They say you're in charge of this wee village, mate."

Takeo nodded his head and bowed slightly.

"Well great, then," said Kelly. "You and I need to strike up a deal and do it quick."

"What type of deal did you have in mind, Mr. Wallaby?" asked Takeo.

Kelly grinned.

Maybe he doesn't like Mr. Wallaby.

"It's easy, alright. You and the people of this village are going to help us with our excavation of those ruins over there." He pointed to the remnants of the Kyoto skyline in the distance. "And you're goin' to give us your village."

"Why do you need our village?" shouted one of the villagers.

"It's goin' to take us a tick longer than we thought to find the treasures below Kyoto and we're tired of living out of our backpacks. Dining on rations. Drinking recycled urine, when the recycling machine's actually working. This seems like a perfect temporary home for us," Kelly said, one corner of his mouth turning upward. "And you lot seem like a good temporary workforce while we catch up on a little R and R."

"And we give you all of this in exchange for what?" asked Takeo.

"In exchange for us not killing you," said the Death Wallaby smugly. "See that guy over there?"

One of the Mongolians peeled away from the pack. He aimed a cylindrical tube connected to a backpack at one of the buildings surrounding the plaza.

"If you resist," Kelly continued, "he's goin' to do this."

The Mongolian let loose a fiery gust at the wooden structure. In an instant, the entire roof was ablaze. The townspeople gasped, or screamed, or a combination of the two; many fled to their homes. The Death Wallaby and his troops laughed hysterically at this sight.

"Run my little chickies, run," cackled Kelly. He returned his gaze to Takeo. "So, as the one in charge of this place, are you in agreement with our proposal?"

Takeo felt his wife burrow her face into his left shoulder. In his right hand was his katana. He thought about how many times his ancestors had stood up to enemies, even with odds as long as those that faced him now.

His thoughts halted. He realized that he had extended his sword towards the Oceania Coalition force.

"Takeo, what are you doing?" whispered Ayuko. "Don't pick a fight with these guys."

"I'm sorry, I didn't mean to. The katana just moved itself and—"

Kelly cut him off. "You're going to fight me with that shiny butter knife, are ya'? Fine then, I'll blast a hole in you and your missus. And send this entire village up in flames."

The katana was still extended.

"Put it down, Takeo," pleaded Ayuko.

Villagers began to cry out, "He's not in charge!"

The pendant that Takeo had discovered in the river, which

he had fastened above the hilt of his blade, started to pulse. The glow flickered faster and faster.

A fan of radiant silver light shot out of the sword and engulfed the Oceania Coalition forces. There were no cries of pain. There were no shrieks of agony. As the light returned to the mysterious pendant on Takeo's katana, there was no Death Wallaby or Mongolian flame thrower or fidgety Vietnamese soldier. There was no Oceania Coalition.

CHAPTER 11

THEY'RE GOING WHERE?

"D ALLAS WAS RIGHT, THAT SHIP had some giddyup."

Ishiro'shea's wink confirmed that he agreed with the bounty hunter's observation.

"And I'm just glad that they hadn't shut down that portal station outside of the Tardasio System. Otherwise, we might not be here in the nurturing bosom of my love."

The ninja shrugged, but Duke knew that Ishiro was as happy to be back on board the *Deus Ex Machina* as he was. Duke Dallas' card had worked like a charm at the casino; the attendant hadn't even batted an eyelash at the two men asking for their ship. And then they were away from T'ckuvu Prime and heading towards Cyborg Joe's. With Hefty Senchax controlling the portals in and around T'ckuvu System, they made the decision to head to friendlier space before making the jump to Kelt. The gang boss might not believe that his right-hand man had not only let them escape, he had provided the escape pod.

"I mean, I know Hefty's ship was bigger, more modern, had way cooler weapons, a better caterer, and didn't sprout cryptic red buttons when in danger…" Duke paused. "Never mind, lost where I was going with that."

His companion shook his head and went back to plotting the course out of T'ckuvian space.

"Oh hey, look." Duke pointed at a blip on the control panel monitor. "Is that a station? It is. And it's outside of Hefty's reach, I bet… and way closer than trying to head over to the next system. Who knows if the Four I's don't have that guarded, anyway? This could be our ticket, Ish."

Ishiro'shea plotted the course to the wayward station. It was a short trip in the *Deus*; despite her age, she could still move when she wanted to. The ship approached the portal, which appeared to be in working order. The station sported the appropriate DIPS insignia, and off to the side was a toll booth. Duke assumed that the booth housed an unyielding android that had had its customer service programs erased, as was the case with most he'd encountered. The Department of Intergalactic Portal Stations was one of the last vestiges of an attempt to implement an all-powerful cosmic government. Like all of the efforts before and after, it had failed, but the DIPS infrastructure remained. An enterprising business-woman from Oscavia paid a large sum of money to the collapsing government to buy the network of stations. Her decision to privatize the only easy way to get from one sector of the universe to the other in mere moments rewarded her with a much larger sum of money.

"Before we drop in on what could be a war zone, let's give Queenie a call," Duke suggested.

After some swift movements from Ishiro'shea's dexterous fingers, the control panel buzzed.

Queen Joe appeared on the forward monitor. "Duke, Ishiro'shea, we haven't heard from you in a while."

The window of her office provided a clear view of the bar. As she spoke, Duke's eyes wandered to it as he tried to see if there was anything afoot. It seemed like a normal day at

Cyborg Joe's. If they were under attack, they were taking it well.

The Queen noticed Duke's roaming gaze. She turned around to peer at her patrons. "What? You see something?"

"Oh no," Duke said, a bit flustered, "I was just seeing if y'all were burning alive at the hands of the Four I's."

"No, they haven't come back since the BHU bailed us out. It's been pretty quiet, to be honest. Well, except for one thing. I'm glad you reached out, actually."

"Before you get into that—because I'm sure it's just going to make our day—aren't you going to ask us about Ishiro's parents? If we found LePaco?"

The Queen hesitated for a moment. "No. I think I know the answer to that. That's the 'one thing.'"

Duke dreaded what was about to come out of the Queen's mouth.

"You aren't going to like this," she began. "At all."

"Go on. It can't be any worse than what we've been dealing with."

"So, you received a message. More like a messenger. Here at the bar."

"Who?"

"Maxx Gemstarr."

Duke turned to Ishiro'shea. "What does that jackass want?"

The ninja's eyebrows tightened; he looked as confused as Duke.

The Nova Texan turned back to the Queen. "What did that jackass want?"

"He had some information that he wanted to give to you."

"This ought to be good."

"Look, Duke, I know you don't like him, but he was being sincere. He actually had something that could help us."

"What? An autographed eight-by-ten headshot? A copy of his latest direct-to-home romantic comedy?"

"He knows where LePaco is. Or, rather, where he was heading."

"Bullshit," Duke blurted.

"I believe him," the Queen responded.

"You don't know that buffoon like I know him," countered Duke. "He only thinks about himself. He has an angle, I know it."

"He wanted me to tell you that he's paid his Bounty Hunter Union dues. All of them. Including back payments all the way to when he thought it was just a scam. He heard what happened here and wanted to thank you for opening his eyes."

"It's an angle."

"Let's assume it's not," the Queen replied. "Can you do that for me?"

"Sure, why not?"

"He wanted to tell you that he's been chasing Mazilda Cloax."

"Why?"

"He said he owes her some payback. And that it sounded like you do too. He thought that with both of you on her tail, she wouldn't escape again. He tracked Mazilda and LePaco for some time—but then decided to pause his pursuit and come here to find you."

"And why was that, pray tell?"

"Because they were headed to Earth."

The bounty hunter fell silent. He sat down at the control panel next to Ishiro'shea, utterly perplexed.

"They're going *where*?"

"Earth," Queen Joe repeated.

"Why? What's there?"

"I'd assume Ishiro'shea's parents and the Amplification Key."

"Did he say if they were headed there by their own choosing or if they were being pursued and chased there?"

"Why do you ask?"

"Back on Psitakki," Duke began, "we ran into an Earther that was on their trail. He didn't have all the answers but he was after 'em. I was curious if his bosses actually caught LePaco."

"His bosses?"

"Yeah, he was an Irish gang punk. A heavy hitter in the Nipponese-Gaelic Gang Wars on Earth. Maybe they ran him down."

"I don't think so. It didn't sound like it," said Joe, "but I didn't ask him directly. Anyways, he left shortly after his message. I'm assuming he's headed towards Earth."

"I guess that means that we aren't coming to see ya' after all. We're going to Earth. Fun."

"Good luck, Duke."

"Oh by the way, Queenie," started Duke. "The Orb…"

"Yeah?"

"It took us to the wrong 'father.'"

"What do you mean?"

"It's of no consequence, but—" Duke paused momentarily. "—just be more careful next time."

A sly smirk, equal parts intrigue and confusion, crossed Queen Joe's face. Then she cut the transmission.

"Ready to go home, Ish?" said Duke.

The ninja sat motionless and expressionless.

"Welcome to Warp Station and Portaling Center #808, I am Department of Intergalactic Portal Stations representative L44-RF47249. You can call me Alejandro. We are very excited that you chose to take our portal directly to Earth, Mr. Lafayette LaGrange. Your funds are sufficient for this jump."

"Thanks."

"Are you sure?" asked Alejandro after a moment's pause. "Like positively positive sure?"

His voice showcased a surprising amount of inflection and personality. For a robot whose entire existence was to perform the most menial of tasks, he seemed oddly concerned about the concept of anyone *choosing* to go to Earth.

"Yes. Earth."

"Good luck to you then," the cybertronic toll taker remarked.

The portal opened and the *Deus* slowly approached.

CHAPTER 12

WHISKY CAKE

THE SPACE AROUND EARTH WAS clear. There were a few transport shuttles entering the atmosphere from neighboring systems, and a fairly long queue from the portal station but, by and large, it was a pretty quiet day around the typically loud blue planet. If Admiral LePaco and Mazilda Cloax really were on Earth, they had arrived without a legion of Four I's ships to protect them. And that seemed odd.

"You don't think Gemstarr was messin' with us, do ya'?" asked Duke. "Sending us to Earth and subjecting us to everything that can happen down there is pretty cruel. Even for him."

Ishiro'shea did not respond.

"Sorry, no offense. I know it's technically your home," added Duke.

The ninja continued to check the scanners silently, without acknowledging his friend.

"It's not like you've lived there in the last decade," Duke said under his breath. Ishiro'shea clearly heard him, however, and shot back a menacing scowl.

"Sorry, sorry," Duke pleaded. "You know Earth and I

aren't best friends. Outside of finding you there, it just seems like a big mess to deal with. But I'll keep my thoughts to myself."

After the *Deus* cleared the checkpoints at the portal station alongside the dead planet Mars, it inched out until Earth became visible. The planet glowed bright blue, its massive continents emerging from their oceanic barrier like they were gasping for air. From this vantage point, there was no evidence of the wars that had crippled the planet. *It looks almost peaceful*, thought Duke. And peaceful was a word that hadn't been used to describe Earth in many, many cycles.

Since the time that Ishiro'shea had left, the Nipponese-Gaelic Gang Wars had spread out and consumed most of the planet. The planet's capital—New Tokyo, Ireland—was one of the most dangerous places in the universe. If you weren't killed by the copious amounts of violence from high-grade military installations, you would be murdered by the inhabitants, hardened by countless cycles of unending bloodshed. It wasn't a pretty place.

Both the Irish and the Japanese had a huge presence in New Tokyo; it was the origin point for the conflict and, indeed, one of the roots of it. Both groups declared legitimate claims as the rightful owners of the area and its history—and, most importantly, its resources. From this quibble had been birthed a planet-wide conflict that had consumed nearly every race and government on the planet. Despite being one of the more developed, if not a tad unusual, civilizations during the early advent of space travel, Earth confounded alien outsiders due to its independent network of governments. This country over here believed *this*. This one over there believed *that*.

The situation was considered wildly unorthodox amongst the other major planetary systems that made up the nexus of advanced civilizations. However, over time, the entire universe began to model itself after Earth's success. The original clamor to have massive governmental bodies to oversee an almost infinite number of planets faded away. The prevailing opinion became: *Everyone do what you want to do and don't encroach on anyone else's turf... and don't get pissy if they're doing something totally different than you.* The only issue was that Earth wasn't a perfect example to use as a prototype. In fact, it had a long history of people not obeying the rules and minding their own business. The small blue planet had more world wars than most galaxies had worlds. Had Earth been introduced to some of these founding races and civilizations during one of their conflicts, the trajectory of the known universe would have been altered. But it hadn't and it wasn't.

Duke, having been reared on a colony of Earth, Nova Texas, had been taught a good amount about its history during his primary school days. He couldn't remember exactly, but there had been around twenty wars that had engulfed the majority of the planet's population. The Nipponese-Gaelic Gang War was number twenty, or perhaps twenty-one. It had left an indelible mark of inexcusable but totally avoidable horror upon the troubled planet.

"Where to, little buddy?" asked Duke. "Where on this mixed-up world should we head?"

Ishiro'shea highlighted an area on the screen. The image zoomed in, to display a smaller area on a tiny island.

It read: *Ireland. New Tokyo. Demilitarized Zone. Aintin Kuniko's Bakery. 4.85 stars out of 5. 3,485 reviews. $$/$$$. Casual. Does not take reservations. Known for whisky cake.*

"This whisky cake better be good," muttered the bounty hunter.

"Quaint," remarked Duke. "They didn't get all those stars from ambience."

The two bounty hunters sat at a circular booth in the

center of the café. The wooden table appeared to be hand-crafted. Two large divots graced its top.

"Or the decor," added the Nova Texan.

After a few minutes, Duke stood up and motioned towards a waitress.

"Or the service."

The elderly lady approached. Her skin was gnarled and weather-beaten; it must have been heavy, because she could barely manage a smile when she tried to take their order. Duke assumed that she had eyes but there was no telling on account of the copious amounts of excess wrinkles. Bald spots covered much of her cranium and she had just given up on the follicles that remained.

"What's the order?" she asked through a toothless half-grin.

"We'll just have two whisky cakes for now," replied Duke.

The waitress didn't say anything, but her disgusted look suggested that she could have guessed the request without having asked. She marched to the back of the café. Duke heard her muffled shouting at some poor line cook in the back.

This must be a really damn good cake, thought Duke.

Duke turned his attention to Ishiro'shea, then scanned the establishment.

"And you think we'll find something here? It doesn't seem likely that these old-timers know much—at least, not about what *we* need. We need a source, someone on the inside."

The ninja motioned for his partner to calm down.

"You know I hate being patient," mumbled Duke.

The waitress returned and forcibly slung down two plates. In the middle of each dish was a morsel that looked as if it had leapt off the cover of the *Oscavian Encyclopedia of Culinary Styling and Edible Art*. It sported a dark hazelnut perimeter and a center the color of desert sand. It looked moist. It looked fluffy. It looked delicious.

Duke pinched off a bit and tossed it into his open mouth.

He didn't bother to chew.

"Good?" asked the aging server.

"More than good," Duke said, despite having a mouth full of the tasty pastry. "*Life-changing* good."

"Want anything else?" she growled.

"Actually, yeah," Duke began, but Ishiro'shea shot him a piercing glance. He responded with an overly stylized mimicking of Ishiro's earlier calming motion. The ninja's brow knitted together.

"How long have you been here?" Duke asked the waitress.

"At Kuniko's?"

"No, here, in this area. The greater New Tokyo metropolitan area, as they say in these parts."

"We don't say that."

"In New Tokyo then. What, forty, fifty cycles?"

The wrinkles in the woman's face converged in her attempt to convey an expression conveying shock.

"How old do you think I am?" she cackled.

Maybe that expression is "appalled," concluded Duke.

"I didn't intend to be rude," he responded. "There's a reason for my inquiry. I'm looking for someone that can help us figure out a few things around town."

The waitress remained standing, her mouth open. She finally dropped her tray and sprinted to the back.

"What'd I do?" Duke asked Ishiro'shea, who shrugged his shoulders in response.

A short man in a dapper business suit approached their table. He wasn't elderly but it was clear that his youth was far in the rearview mirror.

"Excuse me, friends," he began. "I think that you might have insulted that server."

"I see that," Duke replied, "but I have no idea how. I just asked her how long she's been here. It's a pretty textbook question in the field of small talk."

"Oh yes, no doubt, my friend. But—and I apologize for

overhearing your private conversation—that particular young lady is only twenty-five cycles old. And I think you offended her by assuming that she was much older."

"No way," shouted Duke in disbelief. "No way. I don't believe you."

"I know, it is very hard to understand, my friend. But it is true."

"How? Why?"

The gentleman put his hand gently on Duke's shoulder.

"Those that live here have very rough lives, my friends," he said softly. "Those that survive experience more than most entire generations experience. And most of it is bad, very bad, my friends. This place is at the heart of the war. Why people who have the means to leave and choose to stay here is beyond me, my friends." His face grew solemn, his eyes glassy. "Outside of the whisky cake, of course," he said, shrugging off the sadness that had appeared to be consuming him. He chuckled.

Duke reciprocated. "Yeah, it's a pretty damn good cake."

"I'm glad you like it. I've been coming here for as long as I can remember. Do you mind if I join you?" asked the man.

"By all means," said Duke, "we would love some company."

The old man gently slid into the booth next to the Nova Texan. He was glowing.

Clearly doesn't get much company, thought Duke.

"The name's Duke," the bounty hunter said. "This here's..."

He paused. *Oh shit, I can't give us away. What if he knows Ish's name?*

"...Ichabod," he finished, reluctantly.

The ninja shook his head in disbelief.

"Hello, Duke and Ichabod, my new friends," replied the old man. "I'm Eiji. Eiji Otsuka."

"You're Japanese? Like *real* Japanese?" asked Duke.

Ishiro's eyes widened. He then thrust his head into his

open palm.

Clearly that could have been a bit more tactful, Duke concluded.

"Yes, Duke. From an old Japanese family. My roots are on that ancient island, near Kyoto, but I came here as a young child. When the war came, I stayed. I was going to wait it out." Eiji chuckled at his obvious misjudgment. "But I was off about how long the conflict would last, my friends. Now I'm too old to leave. For better or worse, this is home."

"At least this demilitarized zone is safe," Duke remarked. "Well, safe-ish."

"Yes, it was always my dream to live in a demilitarized zone," Eiji retorted slyly.

This old codger is pretty spry, thought Duke.

"It's okay, my friend. It's not all that bad. Aintin Kuniko's is here. And the people in this area are tough, if not inspirational. In the epicenter of humanity's worst, they are humanity's best. They are resilient and hopeful; how many can say that they've spent as long as I have living amongst this kind of Earther?"

Duke and Ishiro'shea didn't respond or counter Eiji's statement. How could they? This aging Japanese man saw elegant beauty and found unfindable good in living between two warring factions engaged in one of the bloodiest conflicts in the bloody history of a bloodthirsty planet.

Luckily, Eiji spoke before they were required to reply. "Why are you here visiting our sliver of paradise? Looking for someone?"

"Oh no. Definitely not," blurted Duke. "We're just here…"

"Yes?"

Damnit, we should have come up with a good excuse, Duke realized. "We're just here because we're fans."

"Fans? Of war?" asked the confused geriatric.

"Yeah, well not of war, per se," rambled Duke, "but of history. Of Earth history, to be exact."

"You're researchers? Like from a school? Or writers?"

"Not as such. Just fans of this crazy little planet."

"You two aren't from Earth? He sure looks like a Japanese ninja," Eiji said, pointing at Ishiro'shea.

"Oh no, are you kidding? Him? Ichabod is much too clumsy to be a real ninja. He's just a big fan."

"And he decided to dress up?"

"Yeah. He's really pumped to be here," Duke said. He didn't have the guts to make eye contact with Ishiro.

"I guess a real ninja wouldn't be seen in daylight anyways. And not wearing green," concluded the old man.

"Yeah, I know, right? A green ninja? That's rich." Duke definitely had no plans to look over at Ish now.

"Where are you from, then?" asked Eiji.

"Uh," Duke stammered, "I'm from Nova Texas. Ichy here is from Kelt. Ever heard of it?"

"Everyone has heard of Nova Texas, my friends. Though I'm afraid it doesn't have the best reputation here."

"Understandable," replied Duke. "And Kelt?"

"We only know of it as it pertains to Cyborg Joe's Grill N' Go & The Why Not Saloon."

"Understandable," repeated the bounty hunter. "It's a pretty glorious place. What this place is to whisky cakes, Cyborg Joe's is to most forms of booze."

"Sounds delightful. Do all people on Kelt—and Nova Texas, for that matter—care this much about Earth politics?"

"I think we're in the upper echelon of passionate Earth-ophiles. We're particularly interested in the Father and his wife, Yumi Flaherty. And their role in this conflict, of course."

"You *do* know your history," said Eiji, clearly surprised. "Such a specific interest, too."

"Yeah, we're what you call micro-enthusiasts."

"I know of them both, of course. But we refer to her as Yumi *Nobunaga*-Flaherty."

"In your opinion, as a resident, what happened to them?

Do you think that they could still be around?"

Eiji brushed off the question as if it was almost too silly to ask. "Oh no, no chance, my friends. They left early on, when their young son was killed."

Say what?

Duke's jaw hit the ground. Ishiro'shea squirmed uncomfortably in his seat. Beads of sweet streamed from under his mask and rolled off his eyebrows.

"I guess I wasn't aware that they had a son that was—" Duke gulped. "—killed."

"Yes, a young son. Apparently the two sides pressured them both to join the war. Father Flaherty was already a leader amongst the Irish. He was a former military man. I heard he was ruthless. The sweet Yumi was a descendent of the legendary warrior, Takeo Nobunaga. Do you know him?"

"I do. The Heart of Nobunaga and all that stuff," Duke boasted, as if he had been aware of the story from childhood.

"Right, my friend. The Japanese wanted her to support their cause because she was the last symbolic tie to the great hero."

"But both opposed the war."

"Yes, I know Yumi did. Not sure about that Irishman she decided to marry." Eiji now displayed vitriol for the first time. "But, anyways, something happened and their son was killed. My money is on those beer-guzzling thugs. Only they would put an innocent child in harm's way."

He might be a bit biased, realized Duke.

"That's very interesting. So, after their son died, they just vanished."

"Some people think they died. They couldn't believe that these two would abandon their people, even if they disagreed with them. When they left, the war escalated to the level it is now. No one has held the advantage for more than a few days at a time. It's a very evenly-matched contest of murder. It can only end in mutual destruction."

"A 'contest' that now extends to every corner of the planet," added Duke.

"Exactly, my friends. Exactly."

"This is fascinating. Thank you for this firsthand testimony, Eiji. Can we buy you something? Maybe a slice of that whisky cake?"

"No need. You may have guessed, but I don't get to talk to many new people these days. This week has been truly extraordinary."

This week?

"Have there been other Earth history buffs like us visiting Kuniko's?" asked Duke.

"Maybe not as enthusiastic as you two—she wasn't in costume or anything—but she was better looking." The corners of Eiji's mouth shot upward. "I definitely wouldn't kick her out of bed. But she didn't offer to buy me a slice of cake, either. So, we can say you're even."

Mazilda.

"It's funny," the aging diner continued. "She was also interested in Yumi and her husband. I told her that she should try the college on the edge of the zone if she wanted to research them further. The headmaster there is one of their oldest friends. I'm assuming he's still around; he's older than me, if you can believe that."

"The College of Cohorts, Consorts, Co-Conspirators, and Other Assorted Sidekick Types?" asked Duke.

"That's the one. Impressive. You have to be one of the only off-worlders to know of that place."

Before Eiji finished his thought, Ishiro'shea was already sprinting out of Kuniko's.

"Sorry," said Duke. "He's really excited about research."

"I can see that, my friend."

Duke tossed a few bits of currency at the old man. "Enjoy the cake."

CHAPTER 13

BACK TO SCHOOL

O N THE EDGE OF THE New Tokyo Demilitarized Zone a cozy grove of trees nestled atop a grassy plateau. To say it was out of place was an understatement. A perimeter fence peeked through behind the first line of trees; behind that, a winding path led to a large red brick structure surrounded by clusters of buildings of various sizes but of a similar style. The property was only a stroll from Aintin Kuniko's, or in Ishiro'shea's case, a frantic sprint.

"Hold up, Ish," Duke shouted between pants. "If she's in there, you'll want backup."

But the ninja kept running until he ran out of real estate. Duke caught up with him at the iron gates. A brick arch rose above the gates; carved into a stone inlay shaped like a setting sun were the words: *College of Cohorts, Consorts, Co-Conspirators, and Other Assorted Sidekick Types.*

Ishiro'shea drew his katana. He raised the blade and brought it down upon the gate in a diagonal strike. The noise was piercing. Sparks exploded from the point of contact. But the gate did not budge. The ninja approached it and examined the strike point. Nothing. Not even a scratch. He repeated the action again, this time adding a battle cry rich with pain and force. The scream contributed nothing. He tried a third time. Duke grimaced: his friend's frustration was palpable. Ishiro tossed aside his katana and charged the gate; he leapt into the air and connected with a *yoko tobi geri* to the padlock. The gate barely rattled.

"Hey, slow down there," Duke said, kneeling beside his visibly shaken partner. "There has to be another way in."

Duke peered around at the seemingly never-ending fence. He felt a gentle tug on his back. He turned around and Ishiro'shea was standing a few paces behind him, holding Ol' Betsy.

"Drop it, Ish," he belted. "Have you ever even fired—"

That unforgettable bellow rang out, echoing around the grove. The blast sent Duke to the ground; debris from the explosion fell from the sky like jagged rain. Ol' Betsy emitted a second boom. The bounty hunter looked up. Ishiro'shea had been knocked to his feet by the unexpected kickback of the sonic shotgun. Duke smiled.

The Nova Texan brushed himself off and turned to see if Ishiro had done any damage to the gate. It remained intact. Betsy hadn't even bent it. However, being a bit of a novice when it came to operating heavy artillery, Ishiro's aim wasn't as precise as his accuracy in wielding a blade. One of the shots had missed the gate entirely and had hit one of the brick pillars that supported the grand archway—and it was now scattered about the lawn. With the column removed, the edges of the impenetrable gate were now exposed, leaving a wide enough gap for Duke and Ishiro'shea to sneak through. The arched sign that sported the college's lengthy name remained intact, miraculously balancing on the damaged support with only a subtle wobble. The bounty hunters hastily made their way through the newly-created doorway and started down the path towards the school.

The campus was eerily tranquil. *Class must not be in session*, surmised Duke. The sun was beginning to set and nightfall had already started to consume the tiny patch of green upon which the school rested.

"Any idea where the headmaster might be? Where his office is?" asked Duke.

Ishiro'shea nodded and pointed to the building closest to their position.

"Main Hall. Headmaster's Office this way," Duke read the sign aloud. "Well, I guess that does make sense."

The ninja repeated his nod.

"Okay, then. Let's be careful. Mazilda could still be here somewhere," Duke said as he opened the unlocked door to the main hall. It opened with an elongated whine, a creaky squeal that could only come from an antiquated door attached to an even more antiquated building. Stealthily, the pair made their way along the darkened corridor.

The next hallway was also dimly lit, but as the two turned the corner, it became apparent that the room at the end was either currently or had recently been occupied. The door was ajar and a light flickered from its depths. They sprinted down the hallway and pushed themselves up against the walls to either side of the opening. Duke motioned to Ishiro'shea that he would take the first glance.

Nothing unusual.

Duke pulled his head back from the entrance, and Ishiro'shea followed suit. The ninja shook his head.

"Yeah, it's pretty dark in there. I can't make out much. We need a closer look."

The Nova Texan entered the room slowly, with his laser revolver drawn. Ishiro'shea entered with even less sound. They both remained low to the ground, trying their best to remain hidden in the shadows as they examined the room in more detail. They dodged and ducked the few flickers of light that twinkled in the room, hiding behind wingback chairs, floor-mounted globes, and tiny liquor cabinets. All typical items in the office of a school administrator. After a few moments, two things were clear. They were alone. And the room had been ransacked.

Duke found the light switch and flipped it on. It was a disaster zone. The bounty hunter knelt down and picked up a gold-plated placard. It read: *Master Ishiro Fukudome, Headmaster*.

We're in the right place, at least, surmised Duke.

Ishiro'shea noticed the nameplate. His eyes welled up.

"Wait a second," said Duke. "Were you named after him? I mean, I'm sure there are millions of people named Ishiro, but it's quite a coincidence."

The ninja nodded slowly.

"Drop it!" a voice said.

The first thing Duke noticed was the voice wasn't female. Or familiar. He also noticed that he and Ishiro didn't have throwing daggers embedded in their backs.

It's not Mazilda.

Duke started to turn to face the newcomer, but then a blazing blue beam whizzed by his face. It crashed down on the table next to him, splitting it in two.

This dude has a laser whip?

"Drop your weapons *now*," the voice shouted. "One move and you're both dead."

"I'm not following you," replied Duke. "How can I drop my weapons and not move? Dropping my weapons, by definition, requires movement."

"Huh?"

"Also, if one of us moves, you're going to kill both of us. That doesn't really seem fair."

"What? Shut up." It was hard to tell if the man was confused or annoyed. Or a little of both.

"Seriously—what if my friend over there moves? You're going to kill me, even though I followed directions perfectly. That's pretty ruthless. Conversely, if Ishiro'shea takes your demands to heart but I'm a tad frisky, he's going to meet that big ninja in the sky. Hardly seems right. You must be quite the coldhearted murderer."

"Did you say Ishiro'shea? As in the Ishiro'shea that attended *this* school? The Ishiro'shea that was the—"

"Salutatorian," Duke interjected. "Yes, the same. But, as you may know, he doesn't talk much."

"Oh yes, a vow of silence. I remember. But I remember his voice from when he first came to the school."

Duke started to slowly rotate. "Is it okay if we turn around now? Or are we going to get sliced and diced by your fancy electric lasso?"

"You can turn around once you drop your weapons," replied the voice. "But slowly. Just because I know who you are doesn't mean I won't kill you."

Duke sighed but placed his pulse pistol and Betsy on the messy floor. Ishiro'shea did the same with his katana.

"Thank you for—kinda—trusting us," said Duke.

The assailant wasn't a large man but he looked as athletic as a gymnast. He wore a blue *shinobi shozoku* but no mask. His face was youthful and his short black hair was matted and unkempt.

Duke looked over at his partner; Ishiro'shea removed the covering over his mouth and smiled.

He does know him.

Ishiro bowed slightly. The man in blue reciprocated the pleasantry.

"It's good to see you again, my old classmate. I would not have thought it would be like this."

Even though the man had addressed Ishiro'shea directly, it was Duke that replied. "We're here to find Master Fukudome. He's in trouble."

The man shifted his gaze to Duke, but then returned it to Ishiro'shea. "What type of trouble?"

No point in lying to this guy.

"There's a very dangerous assassin after him," continued

Duke. "A female. Goes by the name of Mazilda Cloax. She thinks the headmaster knows something regarding Ishiro's parents. It's pretty valuable information."

The whip master twisted uneasily.

"An assassin, you say? Would this assassin have purple hair?"

"Yes!" exclaimed Duke. "That's her."

His eyes fell. "Then you are too late. She has already been here. She has already found Ishiro-sama, I'm afraid."

Ishiro'shea collapsed to the ground.

"Do you know where she went?" Duke pleaded. "What she asked him? What he told her?"

"I do not."

"Damnit," the Nova Texan screamed. "Where is he now? Can we speak to him? He has to remember Ish!"

The man returned his attention to Ishiro'shea. "It's not good, Ishiro'shea-san. The master was beaten severely by this treacherous woman. But—"

"Can you take us to him? We need to find out what she knows. The universe is on the line here, kid."

"For Ishiro'shea, I will take you. I know the master was like a father to him, in the absence of his own parents. I know the master would approve."

Duke exhaled. "Thank you."

"But, let me warn you, he is in very critical condition."

"Understood. Thank you again." Duke paused. "Sorry, I didn't catch your name. And we all know Ish isn't going to tell me."

"My name is Yeop."

"I like your lasso, Yeop."

"It's a whip."

CHAPTER 14

THE MASTER

YEOP LED DUKE AND ISHIRO'SHEA through a labyrinth of hallways and corridors within the college. There wasn't any damage outside of the master's office; the school was immaculately kept, without a speck of dust or dirt to be found. The trio descended a spiral staircase, traveling farther into the innards of the school.

"So, Yeop, you and Ish were pretty good friends back at school?" asked Duke as he made his way cautiously down the poorly-illuminated stairwell.

"I think so. Or I thought so. I think we were all surprised when he took off like he did. In all honesty, we just assumed we'd hear that he found his parents and he'd return. He was such a good student; we were all jealous of him."

"But not the best, huh?" said Duke jokingly. "I mean, he was *only* Salutatorian."

Duke was taken aback when Yeop didn't laugh.

"What are you talking about? Salutatorian is the highest honor."

"What about Valedictorian? Who won that award?"

Yeop chuckled.

"So who was it?" Duke asked impatiently.

"We are the College of College of Cohorts, Consorts, Co-Conspirators, and Other Assorted Sidekick Types. A sidekick could never have the top billing of Valedictorian. That's just, well, it's just silly."

Should've known that one. Shame on me.

"Down here, to the right. That's the master's secret chamber."

"Secret medical chamber?"

"No, just a regular secret chamber," replied Yeop.

"Who's providing the medical attention?"

"No one. A few of us are trying to make him comfortable but we're just staff here, not medical professionals. Master Fukudome said that he that didn't want to be a burden. If it's his time, it's his time; those were his exact words."

"You said he was in critical condition, though. According to whose diagnosis?"

"His. He said he was dying and didn't want help. I thought that warranted the label of 'critical.'"

"Fair enough."

"Let me go in first and let him know that you're here. I don't want to cause further shock as he's not expecting any visitors. Especially a visitor like Ishiro'shea."

Ishiro'shea bowed appreciatively, and it was Duke's turn to give a thumbs-up.

Yeop disappeared into the chamber, closing the door behind him.

After some time, he re-emerged and signaled for the two to enter.

The chamber was a simple box with blank walls and a single overhead light. There were some uncomfortable-looking chairs in the corner and a raised table in the center, surrounded by smaller ones. Candles, providing ample light and fragrance, sat atop each of these smaller tables. All except for one. Upon that table was a weathered brass bowl; spilling over the top were clumps of blood-soaked rags. On the central platform lay an elderly Japanese man. He was covered in an ornate silk sheet but the tattered ends of bandages hung even lower than the beautiful blanket.

Ishiro'shea approached the dying headmaster. The ninja pulled down the part of his mask that covered his mouth. Duke followed, a step behind his companion. He removed his hat.

The old man slowly turned his head until his eyes fixed on his former pupil.

"Ah, Ishiro'shea," he began quietly, "it has been too long."

The ninja bowed.

"I wish it was under better circumstances," Master Fukudome continued, fighting to speak through coughs, "for you and me both."

His stare shifted to Duke. "And who are you?"

"Duke LaGrange, sir. A friend of Ishiro'shea."

The master squinted intensely as if he was trying to look beyond the bounty hunter's physical being and into his metaphysical interior.

"Nova Texan, I presume?"

"Yes, how'd you know?"

"I'm an old man that's been in this universe for a long time. I've encountered many beings and I've learned that Nova Texans have a certain... well, presence."

"Thank you," Duke replied with a slight bow.

"I didn't say it was a presence that people appreciated," the master added with a smirk.

"You got me, sir," Duke said with another respectful bow.

"Well played. I wish your sense of humor would've rubbed off on Ishiro here."

The ninja playfully pushed Duke away. Master Fukudome gave a subtle giggle. He then turned back to his former student. "I'm guessing you know more about what happened to me than I do, Ishiro'shea."

The ninja nodded.

"Who was that woman who attacked me? She was asking

questions that confused me greatly; she was asking about your parents."

"Master Fukudome, sir," Duke interjected, "the woman was Mazilda Cloax. She's an old friend of ours."

"You need to pick your friends more wisely, it seems."

"I don't disagree with you," admitted Duke. "Mazilda is a skilled assassin and is working for a man named Lothario LePaco. He's trying to take over the universe."

"There's always someone," Master Fukudome said.

"But, unlike the others, he has an inside track on how to actually do it. He's discovered a weapon—from another dimension; he has a third of it already—an ancient shield that was on Psitakki. One piece, an orb from a planet called Neprius, is currently under the guard of Queen Joe on Kelt."

"I've heard of this Queen. Some say she is also from another dimension."

"Those people would be right," said Duke. "She is. She's our best hope to keeping the Orb safe. But if LePaco and Mazilda get that third piece—a pendant—then the shift of power might be too much to overcome. LePaco could destroy planets and galaxies with the mere flick of his wrist."

"Fear isn't true power, my friends," said the frail headmaster. "It can only get you so far in the quest for power."

"He also has a massive group that doubles as his army and his middle management. Just as we used to terraform uninhabited planets, he's taking fully-developed civilizations and reforming them into orderly satellite business units, all cogs in the wheel of this new universe."

"This is troubling. And I'm guessing this pendant of which you speak is the Heart of Nobunaga."

Yeop and the teachers bringing new rags and plumper pillows gasped. Duke and Ishiro'shea both acknowledged the master's correct assumption with simple shakes of the head.

"The Heart of Nobunaga disappeared, Master," cried Yeop. "Many cycles ago."

"It did not disappear, young Yeop. When Ishiro'shea's parents left the war, they took it with them. Its power would have only led to even more death and destruction."

"Can there be more death and destruction than what we have now?" asked Yeop.

"Today, there is still hope. Hope that the wars will end. If the Heart was to be discovered, that hope—no matter how insignificant it may seem—would be completely extinguished. Our world would cease to be."

"So it really is magical? It really did do those things that we've heard about in the legend of Takeo?"

"It did, Yeop. It did. But it wasn't magic. It was just an unidentified science that we never fully understood. It seems that it was from a different dimension. A dimension, I assume, that has different laws of nature, and of physics, and of existence."

Duke leaned over closer to the old man. "Master Fukudome," he whispered, "please tell me that you know where Ishiro's parents are. And that they are safe from Mazilda."

The dying master closed his eyes. He shifted his head back to its natural resting position.

"I know where they *were*, but I'm afraid I don't know where they are," he replied softly. "They *were* safe. The Heart of Nobunaga *was* safe."

Duke exhaled. "That's good."

"And I did not tell this Mazilda anything."

"That's even better," replied Duke. "Outside of the physical harm that it caused you, of course."

"It's a risk that we take when we are trusted with great secrets, my friends. But, I must tell you, I cannot promise you that they are safe *now*."

"Why is that, Master?" asked Yeop.

"The assassin did beat me badly. And the beating escalated as I remained defiant to her interrogation. But she did not kill me. She departed suddenly."

"Maybe she heard me coming?" Yeop suggested.

Mazilda wouldn't have run from you—even if you do have a really nifty laser lasso, Duke thought.

"Maybe," replied the master. "A more logical assessment could be that she, or someone that she was working with, discovered Yumi's whereabouts. And thus, she knew where Yumi's husband was. And thus, the Heart."

The room said nothing.

The long silence was eventually broken by a middle-aged Earth woman swinging open the chamber door violently. Her face was white with shock.

"We're being invaded, we're being invaded! They're in our atmosphere," she wailed.

Duke turned to Ishiro'shea. "The Four I's. You stay here with Master Fukudome, Ish. I'll go check it out."

The sky was indeed filled with a Four I's fleet. It wasn't large enough to be an invasion force, especially not for a place as rough and tumble as Earth. For starters, there wasn't an Armada Titan. Earth would surely require an Armada Titan. Of course, the Four I's could have made a mistake and sent the bulk of the fleet to a different part of Earth instead of the military epicenter of New Tokyo. But Duke gave them more credit than that.

I guess the Four I's are going to try and reform Earth, Duke concluded. *Good luck with that.*

A black speck moving towards one of the battle cruisers caught the bounty hunter's eye. It disappeared behind the larger spacecraft. Moments later, a handful of the ships departed the atmosphere.

Holy hedgehogs.

"Ish, we gotta go," shouted Duke as he rushed into Master Fukudome's chamber.

There was no response. No one even looked up at the hysterical Nova Texan. They all remained seated, their heads in their hands, peering at the floor.

"This is urgent," screamed Duke. "That force isn't here to invade. It was here to provide safe passage for Mazilda and LePaco. They have your parents, Ish. I know it."

Yeop stood up and grabbed the bounty hunter's shoulders. His face was wet with tears.

"The master is dead."

CHAPTER 15

THE TRAVELER

THE *DEUS EX MACHINA* SPED away from the New Tokyo Demilitarized Zone and headed towards the southern part of the planet. Luckily, Duke and Ishiro'shea's intuitions proved correct and the Four I's blockade was solely focused around the visible airspace above Ireland. This also meant that Duke's intuition regarding the Four I's primary mission of extraction was likely correct as well. LePaco and Mazilda probably had Ishiro's parents. Even more problematic was the fact that they likely had the Amplification Key.

As the *Deus* exited the Earth's atmosphere, a new problem presented itself—where were they going to find a warp station that wasn't heavily guarded by LePaco's forces? The *Deus'* scanners whizzed and buzzed but there wasn't a beep to signify an identified portal. Nothing.

Then... something. Not a big something, but a something nonetheless.

"Over there. It's faint but it's the best we got, little buddy," Duke proclaimed.

Ishiro'shea tapped on the control panel and the scanning focused on the planetoid.

Delorme. Rogue Brown Dwarf. Uninhabited. Discovered by Earth scientists during the planetary year of 2012.

"Hey, I know that rock" Duke replied, a bit surprised at his own knowledge. "That's 'The Traveler.' It doesn't orbit any star, it just floats around. It's an ugly booger. I wonder why it's registering up on our portal scan. It's uninhabited."

Ishiro'shea typed even faster, presumably diving deep into the bowels of the *Deus'* databank.

The screen overlay transitioned from the basic details to a two-dimensional, animated timeline, starting with the rogue planet's discovery, then entering a long period of absolute nothing, then a little-known fact that intrigued Duke.

Attempted Jungafallowian Colonization.

Duke read the lengthy entry.

"It seems that the Jungafallowians wanted to always be on the move, and what better way than with a traveling planet? How far did they get on colonizing it?"

The screen changed again, citing that the Jungafallowian efforts were abandoned fairly early on when they discovered they had been unsuccessful at altering the atmospheric composition.

"But," Duke began, "if they made a couple of trips to try it, then they had to set up a means to travel efficiently. Like a private warp station."

Ishiro'shea nodded. He twirled his finger around in a flurry of zigs and zags.

"That's right," Duke acknowledged, "it's 'The Traveler.' So, the portal must be attached to the planet somehow. We gotta try it. It might be our only way to Kelt, even though the detour is through Jungafallow."

The ninja plotted the course and the ship sped away from that crazy blue planet known as Earth.

Delorme was ugly. It was rocky, harsh, barren, but mostly ugly.

This would've been perfect for the Jungafallowians, thought Duke.

"What's the composition? Looks pretty rough."

The computer screen spat out pertinent data: *High metal content. Methane atmosphere. Unsuitable for the biologies of 99.63% of known living species.*

"High metallicity. Maybe the warp portal is anchored to the actual planet; it'd be pretty old school, but then again, the colonization was a long time ago," Duke surmised. "Let's increase the scan to the planet's atmosphere."

The *Deus'* scan intensified yet again. The pulsing beep picked up speed; it then morphed into a constant hum and, finally, into a wailing siren.

"We got it," Duke shouted gleefully. "That has to be it."

Upon further inspection, it was indeed an archaic private portal, built as a bridge to and from a distinct location. Unlike the common warp stations that could be altered to take travelers to multiple destinations, this door and its twin were connected by a single, unyielding tube of space-time.

"Looks like we're going to Jungafallow. Let's just hope it's not Jungafallow III."

It was Jungafallow III.

Thankfully, though, the warp portal was stationed in a vast expanse of nothing. In fact, it had probably been abandoned many cycles ago by the ruling Jungafallowian party of the time and then forgotten. But it still worked and that was the important thing. Another important thing was that the Four I's had not approached the Jungafallowian System, so all that Duke and Ishiro'shea had to do was find a more modern warp station and head to Kelt. That was the easy part of this whole imbroglio.

The *Deus Ex Machina* cruised along the outskirts of the system and headed for the space outside of Jungafallow IV. The overly conservative residents of Jungafallow IV would have no beef with an alien ship using their portal because it meant that the aliens in question were leaving. The Jungafallowians on IV were much more intelligent, orderly, and civilized than their crude and overly enthusiastic relatives on Jungafallow III, but that didn't mean that they welcomed visitors.

In between the two primary planets in the system, III and IV, there was a sliver of space occupied with a gnarly asteroid belt. It wasn't the most treacherous gathering of space rocks, but it wasn't a picnic to navigate either. Despite the dangers and obstacles presented by the floating chain of unpredictable cosmic debris, the Trampling Death Robots would routinely hold concerts in the belt, much to the delight of their hardcore followers. One of their better-received albums, *Trampling Death Robots LIVE: But Not If These Damn Asteroids Don't Cooperate*, was recorded on this very same asteroid.

Duke looked at his partner. "It's going to be the fastest way back to Kelt. I've driven through worse. I got this," he said confidently.

Duke was correct in this matter: it *was* the fastest way to the warp station.

With the Nova Texan at the wheel, the *Deus* twisted and dodged, rolled and swayed, as it navigated through the asteroid belt. What should have been a hectic, white knuckle, peek-through-mostly-closed-eyelids moment was rather anticlimactic. It was almost calming.

Duke's focus relaxed once the densely packed portion of the belt was behind them.

"Should be smooth sailing the rest of the way." He removed his hat, sat at the control panel, and let out a sigh of relief.

His attention returned to Ishiro'shea. "I know things have

happened kinda fast, but I want you to know that I'm sorry about Master Fukudome."

Ishiro'shea bowed quickly.

"No, Ish, enough with the stoicism and formalities. I know he raised you. It's okay to be angry. It's okay to grieve some," Duke continued. "I know I'm pissed. I still can't believe Mazilda would do something like that."

Ishiro'shea lowered his eyes.

"You're right, I can't keep thinking she's the same person that we knew back then. I just can't believe it. I promise you, little buddy, we'll get her. We'll get LePaco. We'll find your parents. Nothing can stop us."

As the *Deus* exited the last cluster of rogue asteroids, Duke's mouth opened with no intention of shutting anytime soon. Staring back at them was a ship of behemoth proportions. In big block letters, it read: *TRAMPLING DEATH ROBOTS FAN CLUB & ATTACK SQUAD: JUNGAFALLOW III CHAPTER.*

"Not again."

CHAPTER 16

KISS MY ASS-TEROID

"DO WE HAVE TO PATCH 'em in? I mean we *should*, right? I'm not really in the mood for Jungafallowians," Duke whined, "but it's not like anyone is ever in the mood for Jungafallowians. I don't even think *Jungafallowians* are ever in the mood for Jungafallowians."

As his thought trailed off, his sidekick did the only reasonable thing: he patched them in.

On the *Deus'* primary screen appeared four faces, four necks, and, of course, two Jungafallowians. These faces, however, Duke and Ishiro'shea immediately recognized. Flakka-Grog and Orbo-Terg.

"Oh hey there, guys," Duke began. "Long time no see. I have to say, I didn't expect to see you again. Ever."

"Because you ran away?" the Flakka head asked.

"And you did everything in your power to hide from our vengeance?" added Grog.

"Big wusses!" shouted both of Orbo-Terg's heads in unison.

"No, because I thought you were dead," Duke replied matter-of-factly.

"Well we ain't," blurted the colossal Orbo-Terg.

"You both look pretty close to it."

Duke shook his arm to simulate injury, then grabbed his chest, grimacing in faux pain. Both Jungafallowians looked down at the bandages that covered much of their upper torso. Orbo-Terg's right arm was in a sling; Flakka-Grog's left arm was cocooned snugly in a hard cast.

"These bruises? It takes more than a few scratches from a Gartoshian sneak attack to stop us from completing our mission," Flakka-Grog said confidently.

"Dare I ask what your mission is?" Duke said reluctantly.

"To avenge the Trampling Death Robots and Sprinkles!" Orbo-Terg wailed in agreement.

"How is ol' Sprinkles doing these days? Any more katana blades through the eye?"

Flakka-Grog's faces grew red with rage. "Funny, LaGrange. No, your attempts to kill the greatest musician to ever live—"

"Are we classifying a robot as 'alive' these days? Where exactly do you stand on cyber-sentience? For? Against? Undecided?"

"Stop trying to change the subject, bounty hunter," hissed Flakka.

Duke raised his hands in submission. "Continue, please."

"Your attempts were pointless. Despite the hullabaloo that you caused, the Robots only missed one show. In fact, that's where we're headed now."

"Another one of their asteroid belt shows?" asked the Nova Texan. "Aren't those old news nowadays? I mean, get a new trick, Sprinkles."

Clearly, the Jungafallowians did not appreciate Duke's snark. Their eyes grew fiery and their jaws clenched.

"This isn't any concert. This is the 17th Annual Trampling Death Robots 'Kiss My Ass-teroid' Music Festival, honoring the seventeen cycles since the release of their epic album, *Trampling Death Robots LIVE: But Not If These Damn Asteroids Don't Cooperate.*"

"Any good?"

"Only the best ever!" shouted Orbo-Terg from behind his more intelligent friend.

"Yes, the best ever," echoed Flakka. "And now our festival-going experience is going to be kicked up a notch, because we get to kill you and avenge the Robots without so much as a detour."

"That *would* be pretty efficient," joked Duke. "Tell me something, guys—since you're about to kill me anyways, I don't see why it would hurt to provide a little clarity for an old friend."

"What?" sighed Grog.

"How'd you get the Prince's ship?"

The Jungafallowian rambled on regarding something about trivia and losing money and revenge, but Duke was too preoccupied with a discovery that Ishiro'shea had made on the scanner.

"Good eye, Ish," he muttered. "They're coming here?"

The ninja nodded.

"Just one?"

Ishiro'shea nodded again.

"That's not like the Four I's. Maybe they've decided to organize Jungafallow III. If they're trying to 'improve' Earth, why not Jungafallow III?"

Duke returned his attention to the Jungafallowians; Flakka-Grog was still in the midst of his passionate diatribe and, presumably, his explanation about how he had come to captain the ship of the deceased Prince Korzo-Tapor.

"Sorry to cut you off, big guy," Duke interjected, "but it appears that we have company. Both of us. Four I's."

"Moron, we actually *have* four eyes, so it's not an insult," Flakka remarked.

"Intergalactic Infrastructure Improvement, Incorporated," Duke said, enunciating each word deliberately. "Four I's."

"We know about the Four I's. They've been taking over weak-willed planets. But Jungafallow III isn't a pushover. I've heard rumors that we're negotiating an alliance with them, anyways. Supposedly, they signed some deal on Junga-Mini One last week after they took it over. So, I'd wager they're here for you two. You aren't exactly known to have a ton of allies."

"That does make sense. Maybe you should ask, since you're so buddy-buddy with 'em?"

"What?" Flakka said, surprised.

"They're right behind you. Ask 'em."

Immediately, the Jungafallowians cut their transmission to the *Deus*.

The ship that was approaching the Trampling Death Robots Fan Club vessel was definitely a Four I's build. It was larger than their typical scout fighter but nowhere near the size of a cruiser or an Armada Titan. It was clear from its external design that it was built for speed. Its unconcealed weaponry made it equally clear that it was built for war.

"We really don't have time for this, Ish," Duke groaned. "You think we can outrun 'em?"

The ninja shook his head.

"Yeah, maybe the Jungas, but not this ship. Maybe they'll blow up each other? Wishful thinking, I know."

Suddenly, a light show of lasers and explosions cavalcaded across the back half of the Jungafallowian ship. The Four I's unleashed another devastating assault.

I'm guessing Flakka-Grog and Orbo-Terg didn't win these guys over with their magnetic charm and unparalleled wit, surmised Duke.

The Fan Club ship tried to counter, but it was fruitless. Their heavy artillery options were eradicated by the opening barrage from the Four I's. It was clear that the Jungafallowians had one remaining course of action—retreat—and they were trying to do so with all due haste. Their spacecraft dipped and veered to the right; the Four I's vessel did not pursue, but neither did it lessen the assault. Its fire was concentrated on the rear thrusters of the Jungafallowian ship. Before they could have sung the opening lines to *I Want to Smash You, My Binary Baby,* the ship was limping into the asteroid field without the proper propulsion to navigate it safely. Before the Jungafallowians could have sung the second line of the song, the ship was bouncing from asteroid to asteroid like a ping-pong ball hopped up on a sugar high. Before they could have reached the chorus, the spaceship of the Jungafallow III Chapter of the Trampling Death Robots Fan Club was nowhere to be seen.

The Four I's fighter halted its attack. It repositioned to block the *Deus'* escape route.

The control panel blinked furiously.

Why are they hailing us? wondered Duke.

"Patch them in," he said. "But first, get our shields up and every bit of weaponry that we have on this damn ship aimed at that son of a bitch."

Ishiro'shea extended a thumbs-up and began frantically entering weapon sequences.

"Also, Ish," Duke continued, "be on the lookout for a giant red button. We might need it."

The ninja patched in the transmission.

Staring back at them from the primary screen were, once again, two familiar beings. However, these two beings had only two heads between them. It was Sol and his receptionist and better half, Wanda. Okay, maybe only slightly better.

"Duke, baby! How are you?" shouted the overweight Tardasian bondsman. "I recognized the *Deus* on the scanner so I wanted to drop by and say hello. What are the odds? Then I saw that you were in some trouble with those damn Jungafallowians. I'm glad I could be of service."

"You have such a big heart. Were you doing us a favor last

time when you set us up? We flew right into a damn Four I's trap. Or when you sold out to those bastards? That base they built on Tardasio 7 almost killed us too. In fact, it might have killed…" Duke trailed off. He didn't want to finish his sentence. Sol didn't need to know about his family issues. And Duke didn't want to think about his biological father's death at the hands of the Four I's.

"What?" replied Sol, dumbstruck.

"They might have killed some friends of mine."

"Look, look, look," Sol stammered, "I made some mistakes. I got into some bad dealings. But it's over now, I promise."

"Sol, you're in one of their damn ships!"

"This thing? I forgot it's one of theirs, to be honest. It was part of my deal with you-know-who. I get him easy access to T7, he gives me a really fast ship."

"LePaco?"

"Like I said, I made some bad deals. But I'm done with that. I mean, c'mon, why would I have saved your sorry behinds if I was trying to weasel my way into a secret life of lavish safety? Makes no sense, LaGrange."

"Yeah, it does," Duke replied swiftly.

"What are you talkin' about?"

"You got rid of those clowns, not because you noticed that we were here, but because you didn't want them to get better seats at the Trampling Death Robots concert."

"What? That's preposterous. That's way outta left field, even for you."

"Is it?"

"Yeah, crazy town. You might need to get yourself checked out, Duke."

"Sol, I can see Wanda from here. I can see the writing on her shirt: 'I'd Dismember Koalas for Sprinkles.'"

"That's a different Sprinkles, Duke," Sol shot back. "Total coincidence."

"She has a souvenir foam hammer in her hand. You know, like Sprinkles."

The bondsman chewed his bottom lip. It was clear he was trying to think of a cover.

"Her hat literally says, 'My Boyfriend is Such a Big TDR Fan that He Would Blow Up a Ship Just to Get Better Seats.'"

"Fine, LaGrange. You got me. I just really hate those guys. They're loud and obnoxious."

"Then why are you going to their concert?"

"Not the Robots, you idiot, those Jungafallowian fan clubs. They ruin it for everyone."

"We agree there, Sol."

"I didn't want to sell out to LePaco and those bastards, but it was either that or he was going to take everything. Or kill me. Either way, no *bueno*."

"It's fine, Sol. I know what type of stuff you're made of. I'm not shocked."

It was clear that the bondsman misinterpreted the bounty hunter's sentiment; he smiled proudly. "Can we call it even, LaGrange?"

"Sure. Enjoy the concert. And you too, Wanda."

The plump secretary blushed and sunk back behind her boyfriend.

"But Sol, just don't go helping any more maniac wannabe overlords anytime soon. Please. I'm begging here."

"Fine, LaGrange. Where are you two heading, anyways?"

"Joe's. We have to stop LePaco."

"You're a bona fide moron, LaGrange. Ishiro'shea, you okay with this nutjob?"

The ninja replied with a thumbs-up.

"You're both morons then."

"Enjoy the concert, Sol," Duke said.

Ishiro'shea cut the transmission.

"That's the closest we're ever going to get to an apology from that fat bastard."

CHAPTER 17

WE ARE ALL BLOP

PASSAGE TO, AND SUBSEQUENTLY THROUGH, the Jungafallow IV Warp Station provided a much needed spell from the constant nuisances that had plagued Duke and Ishiro'shea since they had been captured on T'ckuvu Prime. Duke's biggest lingering uncertainty was whether they would get to Kelt in time to provide any help in repelling Admiral LePaco. The mystery of the relative tranquillity was cleared up as soon as the *Deus Ex Machina* exited the Keltian Warp Station.

"Holy hedgehogs," Duke gasped, "how many ships do you think that is?"

The ninja's dexterous digits fluttered over the control panel. Instantaneously, the screen read: *Armada Titans – 2. Battle Cruisers – 35. Scout Ships, Attack Class – 117. Jungafallowian Fighter Ships – 6. Tardasian Military Ships – 12. Unidentified Spacecraft with Military Capabilities – 23. Unclassified Craft – 37. Recommended strategy – Computing...*

This oughta be good, thought Duke.

...Leave immediately. Don't even say goodbye to loved ones... Just leave. Now. You have no chance to survive unless you flee.

Duke sighed. *Figures.*

From the formation it was clear that the Four I's fleet was planning on another concentrated assault on Oldish Kelt and, more specifically, Cyborg Joe's. A small portion of the armada covered the exit and entry points on the other side of the planet.

"I'm taking away two things from this situation," began Duke. "Number one... the Bounty Hunters Union and the crime lord partnership did not survive the sneak attack in the Tardasian System—LePaco doesn't seem to care one bit about the Queen receiving reinforcements. We just waltzed through the closest public portal and not a single Four I's ship even raised an eyebrow."

Ishiro'shea nodded in agreement.

"Number two... LePaco has the Key. And this is his big play to get the Orb." Duke scratched his chin. "Which means I forgot the third takeaway: if he gets it, the universe is *done.* Can you try and get ahold of Joe? Maybe she knows something that we don't."

Ishiro plugged away, but the view screen only displayed harsh static. The ninja threw his hands up.

"They've jammed comms, too. Great."

The bounty hunter plopped himself down in the captain's chair. He let out a gasp coated in frustration and wrapped in despair.

"It all ends like this," he moaned. "It's all over, huh? We just got beat, outsmarted, outclassed by that weasel. Not to mention that probably our closest friend that we've ever had killed the man that raised you, will likely kill your parents, and has helped put an end to the universe as we know it. And here we are, with a front row seat to it all. We can't do a damn thing. Not a single damn thing. We couldn't even get through the outer rim of their fleet. There's no way we could get to Cyborg Joe's to try and smuggle the Queen and the Orb out. There won't be a chance to live to fight another day."

Silence reigned aboard the *Deus* for what seemed an eternity. The Four I's fleet was holding steady; it didn't appear that a single shot had been fired. The *Deus* still sat unnoticed—or noticed and ignored.

Ishiro'shea perked up and maximized a scanner on the forward monitor.

The portal had been activated.

"Surely, by now, everyone wanting to avoid seeing a galactic massacre firsthand has been notified to stay away from Keltian space, right?" asked Duke. "So that means our visitor is probably on the ornery side. Let's get our shields up and weapons ready."

The familiar thumbs-up sign was flashed.

Expelled unceremoniously from the portal was a diminutive space vessel the likes of which Duke had never seen. It was no bigger than one of the *Deus'* rear thrusters. It sported no visible markings, had no visible armaments, and, shockingly, didn't appear to have any means of propulsion. One would think something so minute in scale would possess speed and agility, but it showed no signs of these traits either. The metallic ovoid meandered out of the station and approached the *Deus*.

"I know it doesn't look like much, but be on the ready," commanded Duke.

"Hey there, guys."

"What was that?" asked the perplexed Nova Texan.

"Hey there, guys," the voice moaned again.

"Who's talking?" Duke shouted up at the ceiling. "How are you doing this? Who are you?"

He looked at Ishiro'shea, who appeared equally dumbfounded. The ninja's hands were raised but the control panel continued to beep and blink and buzz.

"Oh sorry, wait a second, my apologies," bellowed the mysterious melancholy intruder.

Suddenly, on the forward view screen appeared Blop, a Blop from Blop.

"What... how... why..." stammered Duke.

"Hello there, Duke LaGrange of Nova Texas and Ishiro'shea of Earth," greeted Blop, rather formally.

"You died. Back on Psitakki. How are you—"

The Blop cut him off. "Yes, I did die. Well, one of us died."

Duke just shook his head in disbelief, his mouth hanging open.

"Blop, a Blop from Blop, died on Psitakki," the formless, chewed-bubblegum-esque Blop continued, "and I'm Blop, a Blop from Blop."

"Yeah, you might need to rewind a bit."

"We are all Blop, a Blop from Blop. We all share a single existence. All of us. We are all Blop."

"A Blop from Blop?" added Duke.

"Yes, you got it."

"I *don't* have it," Duke whispered to Ishiro'shea.

"We all share an existence, a being..."

"A hive mind?" asked Duke.

"Something like that. I know what you did back on Psitakki for Blop. That was very kind of you. We don't see a lot of kindness in our collective travels."

"It was nothing," replied Duke, blushing slightly. "But why are you here? I know the Tournament of the Colossal Calamari is tough stuff, but this is on another level. There are two hundred heavily-armed spacecraft out there."

"I know, and that's why I came. We can't let this LePaco get the Orb."

"How do you know—"

"We Blops know a great deal about this dimension, other dimensions, and so on. There are a near-infinite number of Blops, and an infinite number of Blop thoughts. But we happen to like this universe and don't want to see it destroyed. We think that you can help prevent it."

"And how exactly is that, if you don't mind me asking?"

"*You* will have to figure that out. But I can get you to the planet's surface and to the Orb. From there, it's up to you—but you must stop this evil."

Duke had no response. He just stared at the dark, spherical eyes that poked out of the fleshy, fatty, misshapen head of the Blop. It tried to smile.

"Just follow me," the Blop said in a tone that made it impossible for Duke to consider doing anything other than obey the command. "In a few moments, you'll be back with the Orb."

"I trust you," said Duke. "I don't know why, but I do."

"Thank you. Your trust means a great deal to us."

"But I do have one question before we embark on whatever we're about to embark on."

"Go ahead."

"How did you know that we were here and in trouble? Was there another Blop around here, maybe on board one of these Four I's ships? Maybe on Kelt with a really powerful telescope?"

The Blop simulated a human laugh.

"No, Duke LaGrange of Nova Texas. The *Deus* told me."

"Come again?"

"Your ship got in touch with me. All of the Blops."

"How'd it do that? I didn't press any giant red button this time. Did you, Ish?"

"Of course you didn't," answered Blop. "You should really ask your ship."

Blop tried to smile again and, this time, accompanied the action with a slowly developing wink. Duke got what he was going for. Then the transmission ended.

The nondescript, seemingly harmless silver ovoid slipped out in front of the *Deus Ex Machina*. It began to glow. At first, it was a muted yellow. Then a radiant orange. Then it exploded into a sphere of white light, quadruple the size of the ship itself.

In an instant, the fiery ball of Blop tunneled through the heart of the Four I's armada. All vessels in its path were disintegrated. It burrowed through the hull of one of the Armada Titans, setting off a chain reaction of explosions that took down an entire flotilla of scouts, fighters, and battle cruisers.

"I guess we follow that," Duke said to Ishiro'shea.

CHAPTER 18

EVERYWHERE'S A DEATH TRAP

"I WOULD SAY IT'S GOOD to be back but, under these circumstances, well, ya' know, it really isn't."

"Good to see you too, Duke," replied Queen Joe. "We've missed you and Ishiro. As you can see, we've needed every able body and free pair of hands that we can muster."

It wasn't a shock to Duke that Cyborg Joe's hadn't been restored to its usual ambience following the Battle of Oldish Kelt, but it was surprising that after its tenure as a makeshift hospital it had become what appeared to be a war room. There was no mistaking it: Queen Joe was preparing for war.

"Speaking of these able bodies and free hands," began Duke, "you really need to call them off. Send them home. We've come here to help you escape—you and the Orb."

The Queen flashed her perfectly aligned teeth in a wry smile, as if she had been expecting the bounty hunter's plea. "No, Duke. I'm not leaving here. I'm going to fight LePaco and his forces. Here. No running."

Her tone wasn't particularly defiant or harsh. But Joe wasn't nonchalant either. Her statement was a simple, non-negotiable absolute. She was going to stay and fight.

"You can't."

"I can't?" she shot back.

"No, you *can*. But there's no hope if you do. You're essentially giving LePaco the keys to the universe. We can't hold off an armada of that size."

"I see you helped us out with that."

"What?"

"Reports are that you took out an Armada Titan and some of its supporting cast en route to see us."

"You think *we* did that? I wish. I'd feel better about our prospects if we were capable of something like that."

"I see," replied the Queen coyly. "Then tell our ally 'thanks.'"

"I can't. He's dead. He died so that we could get here and take you away. So we could live to fight another day."

"Blop said that, did he?"

"No, not in those exact... Wait, what? How'd you know about Blop?"

"It's not important. But if I know Blop, I'd suspect that he didn't want you to steal me away; he would—or rather, *they* would—want us to stand up against this evil. Head-on."

"We can't, Queen. Please see reason," begged the Nova Texan. "Please."

"Do you not believe in us? I have certain powers that can be helpful in an attack."

"I've seen the lightning and fire and... whatever that stuff was. I've also seen this planet almost get destroyed by a force that was only a fraction of the size of what's up there now, and without an insane lunatic holding both the Shield and the Key. The odds aren't in our favor."

"We also have the Orb. I'd wager that I can harness the Orb on a much higher plane than the admiral can wield his two artifacts."

"I guess, Queen," Duke said with a sigh. "I'll have to take your word on that."

"We also have a very tough and respectable ground force."

"A few bar patrons and some homeless Keltian refugees does not an army make," countered Duke.

"No, Duke—we have *thousands* of Keltians. I've positioned them in bunkers below the bar and around this area. The Four I's have a clear advantage in the air, but we know they want one thing—the Orb—and they'll have to come here to get it. Plus, I have Po'l and Lilly getting them into shape and trained up, and leading the ground strategy."

"They *are* going to die, Queen."

Duke felt a powerful hand on his shoulder. The Queen's attention shifted to the being standing behind him. She smiled.

"I'm sorry to interrupt," said a familiar voice. "But I was told that you might need some help."

The bounty hunter turned around and, without thinking, hugged the hairy behemoth. Ishiro'shea joined the embrace.

"Yvonne! So glad to see you," said Duke. "Queen, this is the Furry Mountain of Moon Colony #1. I've seen her knock out a Mega-Troll without breaking a sweat."

"I'm aware of Miss Angerdlarnek's fighting prowess. It's very nice to meet you, Yvonne. Welcome to Joe's and, to answer your question, we can use all the help we can get. As you can see, we are currently losing the numbers game."

"It was only a few days after Lilly contacted me that the Four I's entered our neighbor system," said Yvonne.

"I'm sorry, Yvonne," replied the Queen.

"Don't be. We're a pretty tough race. But instead of engaging them head-on, we decided to rally our troops and head here. We want to cut off the head of the snake."

"Yvonne, no," began Duke. "Send your people back. This is a death trap."

"Duke, everywhere's a death trap right now. And it'll continue to be until LePaco is dead," replied Yvonne. She returned her attention to Queen Joe. "We have about twenty-five heavy fighters and a few scouts. We also have two trans-ports loaded with ten thousand of the roughest, toughest

Gartoshian soldiers that you've ever seen. We landed on the other side of the planet and await your direction."

"How'd you get past the blockade?" asked Joe.

"Easy. When you've been through as many wars as we have on Gartosh, you pick up a few tricks. We sent some scouts through the main Keltian Warp Station. The Four I's paid us no attention."

"They did the same to us," added Duke.

"They paid us no attention because we were in their ships," continued Yvonne. "We borrowed some that happened to be conducting pre-integration analyses on Gartosh and its many moons."

"Excellent."

"Each one carried the components for an extremely crude private warp portal. It had just enough juice to get our entire fleet to the planet. So we are here and ready to help."

"I can't thank you and your leaders enough," said Joe. "In fact, let's open up communication now. I'd love to get their ideas." She motioned for the anthropomorphic musk ox to follow her into the back area of the bar.

"Earl," shouted the Queen over her shoulder, "tell Lilly to come meet us up here. Po'l can handle the training."

The Glyptodian barkeep nodded.

Yvonne grabbed hold of both Duke's and Ishiro'shea's shoulders. "I'm so glad that we got to see each other again. And I'm glad it's not on that awful Psitakki," she chuckled.

"Yvonne," Duke began, "this is suicide."

"No, doing nothing is suicide. We are here to fight. We know we're going to lose some of the bravest Gartoshians in a generation... but we also hope that they save us from losing future generations. This universe cannot have a supreme ruler of any ilk, especially not somebody like LePaco."

She didn't allow a response as she squeezed both bounty hunters tightly.

"I hope to see you again, when this is over."

The underground training bunker below Cyborg Joe's was far larger than Duke could have imagined. In his head, the bounty hunter had pictured a converted wine cellar or beer basement, with Po'l screaming at scrawny Keltians about how to swing a broadsword. In reality, the bunker was more of a compound that stretched the length of a fleet of spacecraft. And the Queen did not exaggerate: thousands upon thousands of beings—mostly but not exclusively Keltian—filled the cavernous structure.

"How are we even going to find him?" Duke asked Ishiro'shea. "Seems to be a lot of training by different trainers going on."

An aged Psitakki conducted hand-to-hand combat drills with some wide-eyed Keltian teens. Beyond this, a group of magenta-skinned Hilterian soldiers were providing a crash course on laser rifle marksmanship. Hilterian snipers were known as the most prolific in the universe, putting even Duke's renowned sharpshooting abilities to shame. In the far corner, a Sabromm was projecting images of Four I's and Tardasian ships, pointing out their perceived weaknesses. The Sabromm followed this with rotating holographic images of Four I's soldiers, demonstrating how they might engage in combat. The Keltians attending the seminar all nodded in unison.

Duke and Ishiro'shea made their way past drills, talks, and exercises to an annex carved into the back wall of the compound. At a wooden circular table stood Po'l, flanked by a Keltian male and female, two athletically-built Psitakki warriors, a female Hilterian, and a Goother Rat. Duke recognized the Goother Rat: it was Gha.

"Po'l!" shouted Duke.

The Neprian looked up and smiled. "It's about damn time, LaGrange," he yelled back. "Everyone, this is Duke LaGrange and Ishiro'shea."

"Yes, I know who he is," said Gha mockingly. "He's the almighty champion of the Tournament of the Shield."

"Good to see you too, Gha," Duke said, extending his hand. Somewhat reluctantly, the Gurlfian shook it. "How 'ya feeling after the Tournament?"

Gha's hands moved to cover up bald patches in his fur, presumably from when he was zapped by Maxx Gemstarr's power gauntlets. It was clear that he was still self-conscious about the blemishes.

"Have the Four I's made their way to Gurlf?" asked Duke.

"No way," snapped the Goother Rat. "I doubt they know that we even exist."

"Then why are you here?"

"I like to fight."

"Fair enough. And who do we have here?" Duke said, extending his hand to the Hilterian female.

"I know who you are as well, Mr. LaGrange," said the Hilterian, batting her eyelashes. "My name is Lutra. I believe that you knew two of my relatives, Turla and Arlut."

Not good, thought Duke. *Whatever I do, don't mention MechaBurgers. Nothing about MechaBurgers.*

"Those names don't ring a bell, I'm sorry," he said. "But it's a pleasure to meet you. And I mean 'meet' as in make your acquaintance. Not 'meat,' like a MechaBurger."

Lutra's eyelashes fluttered at an accelerated velocity.

"Thanks for your service," Duke said hastily. "And these two strapping young bucks?"

The Psitakki duo bowed slightly.

"We know who you are as well," said one of the cephalopodans. "Duke LaGrange—a bounty hunter."

"Oh, were you guys at the Tournament?"

"Yes. And I must say, the way that your bout with Gjrazzel went down wasn't—"

"He's a tough bastard," interjected Duke, knowing full well where this conversation was headed. He turned to the green-skinned Keltians. "And I'm assuming you two know who I am as well?"

They shook their heads and replied, "Nope."

"Wonderful. I'm Duke LaGrange. And this is Ishiro'shea."

"We gathered that," said the male Keltian.

"We really should get back to strategizing," added the female. "It was nice to meet you, Duke LaGrange. Now, if you would excuse us..."

Duke didn't know whether to be insulted or relieved. "Actually, I was hoping to grab Po'l for a minute. We need to chat about a few things."

Before the Neprian had a chance to reply, a slim Keltian interrupted. He was panting heavily. *Must be a scout*, concluded Duke.

"Sorry to barge in, but they're here. They came. An entire warship full of them."

Duke glanced around the room. All faces were frozen, eyes wide and mouths agape.

"I'll be damned," said Gha, breaking the silence.

"This should help our ground defenses substantially," Lutra added.

"Duke, this is huge," Po'l began. "I've never seen one but, from what everyone here has said, we just got a much-needed boost to our force."

"We already know about the Gartoshians," said Duke. "Lilly went up to help the Queen with communications."

"The Gartoshians are here too? On our side?" Gha asked.

"Yeah, ten thousand of them, stationed on the other side of the planet. Even brought a few ships along," replied Duke.

"This just keeps getting better," said the female Keltian.

"But then who are y'all talking about?" said Duke, puzzled.

An erratic clanging noise drew Duke's attention to the back of the compound. The warehouse doors raised, revealing a cave.

That must be the back entrance from the surface, surmised Duke.

Hundreds upon hundreds of armed soldiers marched in perfectly-aligned columns through the entrance. The legion of skeletal warriors stopped their procession and raised their sabers aloft. They let out a collective primal scream that shook the very foundations of Cyborg Joe's.

"To go along with our Gartoshian friends, looks like we have a warship full of Hausen-Ra," stated Lutra.

The eager crowd of amateur soldiers and Keltian refugees rushed around the mysterious Hausen-Ra contingent, showering them with handshakes, hugs, and the occasional kiss.

CHAPTER 19

THE TREATY

"WELCOME TO MAURITIUS, GENERAL NOBUNAGA," said the security officer outside the hangar. "May I take your belongings?"

Takeo handed the officer his unloaded pistol, a tiny satchel of coins, and his wallet, which only contained photos of his family. The security officer continued staring at him.

"You need my sword as well?"

"There are to be no weapons allowed in the room, General. Even your sword."

"This sword has helped turn the tide of this war, son. You do know that, right? This magnificent and mysterious pendant, see it? It leveled advancing Coalition forces. It repelled invading troops. It restored freedom to areas of this planet that were being mistreated and abused by the OC."

"I have heard the stories, General. They are amazing tales, sir."

"Stories? Tales? Is that what they are, Officer?"

Beads of sweat rushed down the soldier's forehead. "I'm sorry, sir. I meant they are great..." He struggled to find the words.

"At ease, Officer," said Takeo, placing his hand on the anxious officer's shoulder. "Here you go. Here's my sword."

"Thank you," said the relieved soldier. "I promise to return it to you as soon as you exit the room."

"I would expect so," said the general with a wink. He marched through the open door into the hangar bay.

Takeo traversed the hangar, making his way to a room guarded by a dozen heavily-armed soldiers.

I hate guns. So messy, he thought as he bowed and acknowledged each soldier in turn.

The room was a plain metal box with no adornments or decorations, just a table and three chairs. It looked as if they had been shrunken down and locked away in a filing cabinet. An overly dull filing cabinet, at that.

"Please sit, General," instructed a lime-skinned Keltian female.

Takeo sat. Across from him was the Czar of the Oceania Coalition, Arlo Sebastian Northcott. The czar's eyes danced around the general's face but never locked on Takeo's gaze. Northcott had clearly seen better days.

"Czar Arlo Sebastian Northcott," the Keltian moderator began, "representing the Oceania Coalition and all of its subordinate territories. Seconded by the Assistant Czar, Arlo Sebastian Northcott, Jr."

"Present and acknowledged," muttered the elder Northcott.

Interesting spin on a family business, thought Takeo.

"General Takeo Nobunaga of Japan, representing the multinational force of Japan, Ireland, the United States, India, Morocco, Poland, Finland, Mexico, Venezuela, Yemen..."

"Present and acknowledged," said Takeo, politely interrupting the Keltian's reading of the thirty-five partner nations.

"And your second, President Dougal Fionnlagh of the Republic of Ireland."

"That's the *grand* Republic of Ireland, my good woman," added President Fionnlagh.

"Very well," replied the Keltian. "Moving on. As all parties should be aware, much of the treaty has already been discussed independently and agreed upon verbally. These proceedings will finalize all elements of the agreed-upon contract and will, hopefully, usher in a new era of peace to this planet. Because, off the record, Earth is somewhat of a laughingstock in our neighborhood. So, let's not screw this up, okay?"

The Earth representatives looked at each other and nodded.

For the entirety of the meeting, both men signed, initialed, and shook hands on each and every point. With the help of some Keltian ambassadors serving as the chief architects, the Treaty of Nobunaga appeared to be a well-crafted springboard to peace for the war-riddled planet. When the last signature from Northcott was inked on the page, the Oceania Coalition was dissolved and the war was officially over.

Takeo stood up, bowed to the Keltian moderator and to his adversary.

"So what are your plans now, General?" asked Northcott.

The general smiled. "Peace, Arlo, peace. That's what we plan to have."

"And how does one achieve peace, General? Do *you* know? I thought I did at one time."

"Peace by brutality and coercion is not real peace," replied Takeo.

"So how, then? Or are you going to make me wait and find out?"

"First, by removing elements of evil," the general said bluntly.

"I guess that's me," retorted the former czar.

"You know what you've done, Arlo. And once those that

are globally recognized as 'bad' are eliminated, we can all be on our merry way. Independence and freedom breeds peace."

"If I may interject," said President Fionnlagh. "What the general is trying to say is that once the allies decide on a strong, fair-minded leader, it will usher in a new era of peace."

"No, President, I didn't mean to say that. I meant to say that every nation can focus on themselves, and figure out what's right for their own people and culture."

"But General, what happens when a great threat like the czar here—"

"*Former* czar," corrected Takeo.

"Yes, like the former czar here, rise up. A bunch of secluded tribes can't stand up against that."

"With all due respect, President, this is not the time nor place to discuss these things."

"Not so easy, is it?" chimed in Northcott. "It all starts with a seemingly insignificant disagreement. And your magic weapon can't help you with this, General. In fact, who's to say that I don't have someone out there trying to steal your precious sword as we speak?"

"That would make me pretty angry," said Takeo. "I love that sword. It's a family heirloom, you know."

"Screw the sword, what about the weapon?" shouted the president. "I'll go look for it. I have my guys out there."

The Irishman dashed to the door, swung it open, and disappeared as it closed with a twang.

"Relax," said Arlo. "I'm not that crazy. How did I lose to you morons?"

"I'm not that stupid, either," replied Takeo with a wink. He tapped his chest, where something made a faint protrusion under his shirt.

"The ol' decoy," smirked Northcott. "Very sneaky."

"Good luck with your exile, Arlo. I hear that where you're going is nice this time of the cycle."

"No, good luck to you, General. Good luck with

convincing those power-hungry politicians that are still on a high from winning the war that they should hitch their buggy to your winning horse. That we should all go back to happy, mind-our-own-business pockets of civilization. You're going to love it."

The former czar and his son exited the room.

"He's right, you know," said the Keltian moderator. "I'm not sure that your brethren believe in independence as much as you do, Nobunaga. They have power in their hearts. Not freedom."

"They will see the light and their hearts will be filled to the brim with freedom."

"I hope you are right, General, I do. And I hope that they get it before it's too late."

CHAPTER 20

HOPE

"Y A' KNOW, LITTLE BUDDY, I wish I woulda said 'no' to Po'l when he asked to come with us. I feel that we just got him killed."

Ishiro'shea appeared to consider this, but offered no sort of indication as to whether he agreed. Duke was used to this tactic, which forced him to review the words that had just left his mouth. On most occasions, some alteration was required to his initial thought.

"But it was his choice," he added reluctantly. "How could we have predicted this?"

Damnit, he did it again, thought Duke.

They walked back into the main bar area of Cyborg Joe's. The Queen and Earl were in conversation behind the bar. Keltians, Hilterians, and a few Psitakki milled about and appeared to be engaged in "war things." The bounty hunters sat on the two stools closest to the Queen.

Joe looked up and addressed them before Duke could ask a question. "Bigger than you thought, right?"

"What?"

"The force. More people came than you thought, right?"

"I didn't really have a number in mind..."

"The Four I's and LePaco's goals mean an end to everyone that doesn't offer up their resources—their people and their freedom—to their cause. We didn't pay these people. We didn't force them into military servitude. We just asked. In some cases, we didn't even have to ask."

"Queen, I'm not challenging the reason that you're leading this resistance. We're part of that resistance, in the larger sense. I'm just saying that a pitched battle on this already-injured planet, with a makeshift, bandaged-together army against a much larger, fresher, and finely-tuned operation isn't the right way to move our cause forward."

"You still think that I should run?"

"Yes. Legions of Hausen-Ra and Gartoshians aren't going to take out two-hundred-plus spacecraft packing the most advanced life-elimination devices," argued Duke. "The Orb is our most precious resource."

"You're wrong, Duke. Our most precious resource is hope."

The bounty hunter rolled his eyes. "You're too good for tired old clichés and motivational tactics. Hope is good. It doesn't win battles."

"Remember when I told you that if something isn't worth fighting for, it's not worth having?"

"I thought it was 'Anything without a cost isn't worth having,' or something like that."

"Close enough."

"I'm not saying that our freedom isn't worth fighting for... Just not fighting for *right now*."

Queen Joe's face scrunched.

"So, why now?" asked the Nova Texan.

"This is my fault. I let these weapons surface, and two of them fell into the hands of someone as dangerous as any Flying Rot. This *is* our best chance—no, this is *my* best chance—to right the wrong."

"Why?"

"All three items could conceivably be in the same place at the same time."

"Which also means that LePaco has the ability to get ahold of the missing piece to his plan for universal domination."

"It is a risk."

"I can't be part of this," huffed Duke. "This is going to get a lot of good people killed. Did you even ask the others if they agreed with this plan? Did you give them options?"

For the first time in as long as Duke could remember, the Queen seemed to not have a retort. As hard as it was for Duke to believe, she seemed flustered.

Cyborg Joe's began to rumble and shake. A chain of ear-bursting explosions followed. Everyone hit the ground.

"Everyone to the bunker," commanded Queen Joe. "This is it—the assault is on!"

"Ish, think we can make it to the parking lot?" Duke yelled. "We have to get out of here. We can do a lot more damage to LePaco from the *Deus*."

He began to head towards the back door but the ninja grabbed his arm, yanking him almost to the ground. Ishiro'shea shook his head.

"We can make it..."

The barrage escalated until there wasn't a single pocket of dead air, just one long, extended *kaboom*.

Duke sighed. "The bunker it is."

Beyond the training stations, the annex of the main bunker was now filled with more people than just Po'l and his colleagues. Duke didn't recognize the newcomers, save the Queen, Earl, and an anthropomorphic musk ox from one of the moons of Gartosh.

"Ishiro'shea! Duke!" screamed Lilly. "They said that you two were here but I didn't know if I'd get to see you."

"I wish it was for a different reason," responded Duke.

"Don't we all. Yvonne spoke very highly of you two. Sounds like that was quite an adventure on Psitakki."

"Without a doubt. What's going on out there?"

"As predicted, the Four I's have begun an assault on Cyborg Joe's—well, all of Oldish Kelt, really—to try and knock out our ground-to-air defenses."

"The joke's on them," interjected Gha, the Goother Rat, "because we don't have any ground-to-air defenses. They're just wasting energy and ammunition."

"Not exactly a sustainable strategy," replied Duke.

Gha sneered and went back to his conversation with the pair of Keltians.

Duke turned to the Queen. "Will this bunker hold?"

"It will, Duke," she replied. "And the other bunkers will hold, as well. When the battle comes to the surface, we will be ready."

"Why would they ever bring it to the surface? They'll just bomb us until we run out of food, drink, or hope."

It was clear that the Queen didn't appreciate that last jab from the bounty hunter. "You think we'll run out of drinks? This is a bar, isn't it?"

The laughter was proof that the Queen had deflected the query perfectly. Before Duke could respond, she cut him off. "Do you think that our entire strategy, which is built around forcing them to face us in a ground battle, was discussed and agreed upon without us having a way to actually *get* them to the surface?"

"Well, no, but—" the bounty hunter stuttered.

"Lilly?" The Queen gestured to the musk ox.

"Yvonne and the Gartoshian force on the other side of the planet will engage LePaco's fleet," said Lilly.

"And get mauled. Lilly, there's no way that two dozen of your fighters can overcome a ten-to-one disadvantage. Even if you take out half of their fleet, they'll just wait until they overwhelm you and resume bombing us down here. I feel this strategy is still without realistic expectations."

"You should really let your friend finish," said Queen Joe, quite politely.

"After our forces engage the Four I's fleet," continued Lilly, "we hope to capture most of their attention. Then our other fleet can enter through the warp station and attack from their exposed rear. This push should force LePaco's hand. He doesn't want to risk getting blown out of space by a rogue attack; he will come to the surface with what he thinks is a superior force."

That does sound better, thought Duke.

"What other force? More Gartoshians?" he asked.

"No, Duke," answered Lilly. "Most of our entire fleet sits on the other side of the planet."

"Then who?"

"When Yvonne came and told us the good news about the support from Gartosh, she also was working on something through her own personal connections," said Queen Joe with a mischievous grin. "Let's just say that her networking has helped us even the playing field."

The monitor on the annex wall blinked and powered on.

"Can you hear us? Is the transmission going through?" asked Lilly.

The screen fizzled; then coalesced into an image. An image that made Duke LaGrange sick.

"Are you kidding me? Maxx Gemstarr?"

"Hey Duke," Maxx said, waving to his rival. "Didn't expect to see you again."

"You lot think that Maxx Gemstarr is going to turn the tide against that armada?" Duke stared at the rebels gathered around the monitor. "Really, Queen? Lilly? Did y'all go crazy?"

Maxx began to laugh hysterically.

"He *did* find a way to circumnavigate the communications jam," reminded Lilly.

"Duke, you are too funny," Maxx began. "Maxx Gemstarr isn't going to turn the tide singlehandedly."

Great, now he's talking in third person.

"Maxx Gemstarr and a really badass group of pissed-off Earthers are going to turn the tide," said Gemstarr confidently.

"Earth?"

"Yes," replied Lilly. "Yvonne reached out to Maxx about helping the cause. Just about that time, he was heading back to Earth to see if he missed anything on his search for Mazilda, but they were fighting off the Four I's, and successfully. He got in touch with some of the leaders and they agreed to lend some firepower to our cause."

"And they just like to fight," added Maxx. "And I think they were tired of fighting each other. We have about fifty of their best fighter class ships—some Irish, some Japanese, some from places that I've never heard of. I mean what type of name is Ghana?"

Not Ghana be around after this attack, Duke mused.

"And Ishiro'shea, I wanted to tell you that your friend, Yeop, said that he'll meet you at Cyborg Joe's when he's done avenging the master, whatever that means."

Ishiro'shea radiated with happiness. His glance met his longtime friend's.

There goes our "live to fight another day" strategy, concluded Duke.

The bunker shook ferociously as the overhead lighting intermittently blinked and lost power.

CHAPTER 21

KILL THEM ALL!

EVERYONE IN THE BUNKER REMAINED silent. Whether this was due to the massive surface assault rendering the ability to converse impossible, or the gathering of thoughts before what would likely be their last moments in this life, Duke didn't know. He did know that opening salvo from the Four I's force was lengthier than he would have liked.

LePaco's not leaving anything to chance, he thought.

He turned to Queen Joe. "It's kinda sad. The end of an era."

"What's that, Duke?"

"If—I'm sorry, *when* we go to the surface to fight these cats, Cyborg Joe's is going to be gone. It's gonna be harder to wrap my head around that than I thought."

"The bar will be fine," the Queen replied flippantly. "It's made of pretty stern stuff. Stuff that you or anyone in this universe wouldn't understand."

"I don't know. I've seen it show a bit of wear and tear over these last cycles, and none of that was anything like an all-out barrage by a fully-equipped armada."

"We shall see," she replied calmly.

"What about the portals?"

"The portals are closed. It's not like LePaco can walk in the front door of Joe's and throw them in the back seat of his spaceship. There's nuance to summoning them and even more to controlling them."

"I know he's not going to *take* them. I just wasn't aware if they could be destroyed," Duke explained.

"They'll be okay too."

Earl wedged himself between Duke and Queen Joe. He wasn't being rude—that wasn't in Earl's nature—he just sometimes didn't have the best spatial recognition.

"Our feed is back up, Queen," he said in a throaty baritone. "We have full-range scanning of Kelt and the immediate space outside the planet's atmosphere."

"Great work, Earl. Let's get it up and we can start to plan our counter."

The bombings were still rocking the bunker but the frequency was finally starting to lessen. It was now possible to finish a complete sentence without being knocked over by a detonation. The Queen and those in her makeshift inner circle —Po'l, Lilly, Gha, Lutra, the Keltian couple, an aging Sabromm called Gerald, and a representative of the Hausen-Ra contingent—encircled the large monitor. Earl, with the aid of three Keltians, hooked up four other monitors to create a workable command center.

What appeared on the screens was shocking, though not unexpected. One of the cameras surveyed the immediate area outside of Joe's and panned up to provide intel on the damage to Oldish Kelt, where the bombings were concentrated. It was barren. Forests demolished. Hills flattened. Buildings toppled. The buildings had already been in a bad way following the Battle of Oldish Kelt, but were now simply heaps of rubble. As the feed showed a wider swath of land, it became clear that the Four I's attack force had not only concentrated its firepower around Joe's—it had totally ignored the rest of the planet. This, of course, was good news for the hidden Gartoshians and any bunker outside of the bombing zone.

"Anything on their fleet?"

The Glyptodian barkeep pointed to one of the side monitors. It displayed a clear view of the armada. Other than the results of Blop, the Blop from Blop and his suicide run to allow Duke and Ishiro'shea to reach the planet, the fleet remained intact and unharmed. The two-hundred-plus ships, supported by a massive Armada Titan, hadn't even broken a sweat.

The primary screen scratched and whirled.

"What's going on?" asked the Queen.

"I don't know," replied Earl. "I think someone is hacking our feed."

Ishiro'shea darted past the members of the inner circle to sit beside Earl. After only a handful of taps, pokes, and keystrokes, the erratic noise stopped. The ninja pointed to the primary screen.

"Or someone wants to say 'hello,'" added Duke.

On the screen, in living color, was Admiral Lothario LePaco. In typical LePaco fashion, he was grinning and plucking his wispy mustache. The beautiful, violet-haired assassin, Mazilda Cloax, stood directly behind his left shoulder.

"Good to see you again, Queen," LePaco began. "Always a pleasure. From the lack of dead bodies showing up on my scans, I'm guessing that you and your ragtag bunch of imbeciles are camping out below ground. That might have saved you from the first bombing run, but by bombing run fifty, I'm not so sure."

"We'll take our chances, Admiral," replied Queen Joe decisively.

"And your people there, you speak for them? Those that are supporting this foolish endeavor—all they have to do is convince you to give me the Orb and this will all be over."

"So you can control the universe?"

"I'll admit, I will have a power unmatched by any being in the history of this fair universe and this fair dimension. Yeah. And it might take some time getting used to planets organized by the good people at Intergalactic Infrastructure Improvement, Incorporated... but you'll be alive." He cleared his throat and straightened his posture. "If you can hear me, everyone," he said in a close approximation to a booming voice, "just get the Orb from this charlatan. She has betrayed you. She has lied to you. Bring it to me and this will all be over. Everyone will be safe."

There was little more than a murmur amongst the people that LePaco claimed were being lied to by the Queen.

Clearly, they are loyal, almost to a fault, thought Duke.

Po'l stepped in front of the Queen. With the formality of a politician, he said, "On behalf of the planet of Neprius and our fearless leader, Ja'a of the Southern Land Mass, we reject your offer, Admiral. We reject your offer and we condemn your actions wholeheartedly."

Lutra, the Hilterian representative, made her way to the front. "As a representative of the peaceful planet of Hilteria, I formally denounce the actions of Admiral Lothario LePaco—"

Before she could finish her statement, Gha the Goother Rat cut her off. "The Goother Rats of Gurlf solemnly pledge their allegiance to the cause of capturing or, preferably, killing the heinous murderer and tyrant, Lothario LePaco."

"For his egregious and unforgivable war crimes and the destruction of much of our beloved planet of Kelt," the Keltian duo said in unison, "our leaders have authorized us to declare Admiral Lothario LePaco a being that should be executed upon capture."

A member of every race represented in the bunker stepped before the monitor, looked LePaco directly in his beady eyes, and denounced his aims, actions, and his existence. What the Queen's army lacked in firepower, it made up for in grit.

LePaco interrupted the stream of those declaring their

opposition to his rule. "Fine, fine, fine. I get it. You don't like me. You don't want me to rule you. So, unfortunately, that means one thing. You're all going to die. And when I'm done here on Kelt, I'll make sure to personally see to the genocide of each of your races. This universe will go on without Goother Rats—for which, I'm sure I'll win some type of award—Hilterians—though I'll miss those neoprene suits—Sabromms, Neprians—and no one will even notice that one—"

His rambling was cut short by Lilly. The Gartoshian musk ox said, "Admiral LePaco. The government of Gartosh and all of its moon colonies has declared open war on you, your allies from Jungafallow III, the Tardasian System, and the Four I's organization."

"Who cares?" blurted LePaco. "Don't you all get it? I don't care. I'm going to kill you all."

Lilly, undeterred by the screaming madman, continued with her formal decree. "As with any interstellar conflict that befalls the Gartoshian government, we offer the opportunity to discuss a truce prior to conflict."

"You're kidding me? You have to be kidding me," LePaco cackled, eyes rolling. "These declarations, or whatever, don't mean anything. You are all going to—"

Mazilda whispered something into the admiral's ear.

"What?" he shouted in response. "We just lost what? How many?"

Cloax began to whisper again but the admiral pushed her away.

"Never mind. It doesn't matter. A few Gartoshian ships are nothing more than a minor hindrance. A nuisance. Remember that, Gartoshian, your ploy is going to accomplish nothing other than seeing the crews on these ships smashed into stardust at my hands. And I'll make sure to push the button myself when I blow up your crummy planet and all of its crummy moons. Kill them all!"

The admiral ended the communication.

CHAPTER 22

DUCK AND WEAVE

A S FAR AS DUKE COULD determine from the makeshift command center in the bunker below Cyborg Joe's, the Gartoshian fleet was more than a nuisance for the much larger Four I's armada. The attackers were focusing on thinning the ranks of the Attack Class Scout ships; their strategy was to avoid the heavier hitters like the battle cruisers, leaving those for the reinforcements. It was an intelligent plan, executed properly.

"Earl, patch in Maxx," requested the Queen. "The Gartoshians have done their part."

Duke glanced at Lilly. Her smile radiated pride. Her people had done *more* than their part; indeed, they might have turned the tide.

The screen continued to flash but Maxx Gemstarr's image did not appear. Normally, this would have thrilled Duke but in the circumstances, it was bad. Real bad.

"What's wrong? Where is he?" pleaded the Queen.

Ishiro'shea joined Earl to try and troubleshoot the issue but the screen just kept crackling.

"I think they're jamming us again," said Lutra, the

Hilterian ambassador. "Maybe they figured out Gemstarr's workaround?"

"This complicates things," said Queen Joe.

The Four I's began to recall their scouts, likely sensing that they were losing more dogfights with the Gartoshians than they were winning. The rebel fleet appeared comically minuscule and insignificant drifting around the massive armada like gnats, trying to lure out ships to engage. With every moment that Gemstarr's invasion force remained hidden, LePaco's battle cruisers came closer to encircling the Gartoshians. The proud musk oxen warriors were slowly being trapped.

This isn't good, thought Duke. *Damn, Gemstarr, show yourself!*

Lilly rushed to one of the side monitors. "Can you get ahold of Yvonne?"

The Glyptodian barkeep, now communications specialist, patched in The Furry Mountain of Moon Colony #1.

"Yvonne, we lost contact with Maxx," said Lilly. "You need to abort and retreat."

"I'm not so sure that's going to be possible. They have us surrounded pretty good," Yvonne replied. "No sweat though, we'll hold them off as long as we can. I'm sure Maxx will figure it out."

"I wouldn't hold my breath," Duke smirked.

The Queen flashed him a nasty snarl.

Wait, did I say that out loud?

"Seriously, Yvonne," said Lilly, "get out of there."

"No. Our mission is to cause problems by taking out as many ships as we can. And we're going to do that. Until we have not a single ship operational."

"You mean until you're dead," countered Lilly.

"We promised a service and we're going to deliver. It's for the right cause. We can't let this maniac take over our universe. Whether Maxx comes or not, we're going to try and force these bastards to the surface. When they're there, promise me one thing, Lilly?"

"Yeah?"

"Punch as many of these sons of bitches in the face as you can. Show them what it means to be a Miss Bovine Boxer."

Yvonne winked as she ended the transmission.

The battle cruisers began to unleash a crippling barrage of firepower on the undermanned Gartoshian fleet, but the brave musk oxen charged as if they were the overpowering force. The battle cruisers picked off many of the advancing ships but the Gartoshians were undeterred. Yvonne and the pilots of three other craft collectively incapacitated a cruiser. Then another. The Attack Class Scouts rejoined the ranks. A few of the Tardasian and Jungafallowian Fighters replaced them at the front line.

The Gartoshians, though valiant, could not withstand the closing fist of the Four I's fleet.

Amidst the chaotic scramble, two ships moved beyond the battle cruisers and headed deeper into the heart of the Four I's armada.

"What are they doing?" asked Lutra. "Are they abandoning the fight?"

"They can't be deserting—that's Yvonne," said Lilly. "She wouldn't—"

Duke cut her off. "They aren't running away, they're running *to* the warp station. They're going to go get Maxx's sorry ass."

The two Gartoshian vessels were cruising through a dense concentration of enemy ships, taking some damage, dealing out some, but they appeared to be mostly focused on getting to the warp station. Unfortunately, a massive battle cruiser stood in their way. And behind it, another battle cruiser.

"They're sitting ducks," shouted Gha. "Those cruisers have their route blocked."

The Gartoshian ships maneuvered into single file and kept pushing at a rapid rate.

"No, they aren't," chimed in the bounty hunter. "They're going to get through."

"How?" asked Lilly.

"In the most honorable way possible."

Yvonne's ship charged the first battle cruiser at maximum velocity. She had the forward armaments on full bore but her intention wasn't to shoot down the more powerful Four I's ship.

She was going to ram it. She was going to sacrifice her life.

"Yvonne, don't—" screamed Lilly, hitting the control panel to try and establish a communications link to her fellow Gartoshian.

Ishiro'shea and Duke embraced her simultaneously. They knew what was going to happen.

The explosion lit up the celestial canvas. It was brighter and more magnificent than any of the plasma cannons or lasers. Yvonne's collision ignited the first battle cruiser, which instantly became a fireball the size of a planetoid, obstructing the view of the second battle cruiser. The trailing Gartoshian ship slipped through the carnage and darted directly for the warp station, with the enemy none the wiser.

Duke immediately thought of Blop and his similar gesture that had allowed him and Ishiro'shea to reach Kelt and the resistance. Yvonne's was equally as magnificent and honorable.

Only a few hard-to-capture Gartoshian ships remained. Their duck and weave tactics were losing their duck and were becoming a tad short on weave. The numerical advantage was now too much. Furthermore, there was no sign that Maxx and his alleged Earth allies had been successfully contacted. As time ticked away, the hopes of forcing LePaco to the surface of Kelt dwindled.

"You don't think that Gemstarr set this whole thing up, do you?" Duke whispered to Ishiro'shea. He looked around to make sure no one had heard him. He didn't want to diminish the already waning morale.

The ninja shook his head violently.

"Okay. If you're that sure, little buddy. I'm with you."

The screen blinked again.

"Maxx!" shouted a Keltian. "It has to be Maxx trying to reach us!"

Earl brought up the visual. Groans echoed around the bunker with as much force as the sounds of the bombing runs.

"Hello again, everybody," chuckled Admiral LePaco. "That was cute. You had me for a second. But, as I was saying before, you are all going to die!"

The image on one of the side view screens caught Duke's eye. He moved in front of Queen Joe to stare directly at LePaco.

"I'll be a monkey's uncle," began the admiral. "Duke LaGrange. I'm surprised that you're still alive, with all the trouble you get into. When I'm done squashing these last few Gartoshians, I'm going to make sure to detonate a few extra special bombs right on top of Cyborg Joe's, in your honor."

The bounty hunter smiled and tipped his hat to the admiral.

The admiral was jolted, crashing to the floor.

CHAPTER 23

MAXX AND THE EARTHERS

D UKE ALMOST FELT BAD FOR the low regard in which he had held Earth until now. They were an advanced race, technologically-speaking, and had been a key player in the expansion of planetary trade. However, apparently, they weren't advanced enough to exit the pattern of major conflicts that threatened their existence every hundred cycles or so. They were the only known civilization that numbered their "world wars" and even added catchy subtitles for dramatic effect. This began as far back as most Earthers could remember: World War II – *The War to End All Wars*; World War V – *South Pacific Rage*; World War VII – *Kings Versus Presidents*; World War IX – *Super Mega Fight Supreme*; World War XI – *Whose God is the Most Right?* The last of these was a fan favorite within the Andromeda Galaxy.

But the cycles of conflict and turmoil must have infiltrated the very DNA of the Earth human, because they were *good* at it. The Four I's forces had struggled with the flightiness of the Gartoshian attack but they regrouped and used their significant numbers to regain the advantage. The Earth force was not much larger than the fleet of heroic musk oxen, but now the Four I's fleet was beyond flustered. The humans' patterns of attack were irregular. Some ships worked in tandem, others engaged independently; there was no leader and no coordination. This confused the orderly Four I's greatly.

Ishiro'shea pointed at the monitor, which displayed a ship that was bulky but agile. It had just blasted an Attack Class Scout with a bright green laser and was turning its attention to a Jungafallowian Fighter. The vessel sported a giant shamrock insignia on its flank.

"Irish?" asked Duke.

The ninja nodded.

"And I'm guessing that one's from the Japanese gangs?"

Ishiro'shea nodded again. Onscreen, a trio of sleek, elegant craft executed a synchronized barrage that sliced a Tardasian ship into tattered ribbons.

Having bought some much-needed breathing room, the remaining Gartoshian ships doubled back and resumed hunting the Four I's scouts.

The most unremarkable ship was a saucer-like pod zigging and zagging through the carnage.

"Zoom in on that, Earl," said Duke. "Where's that little guy from?"

The Glyptodian maximized the image just in time for them to witness the tiny ship's hidden ace. Electric blue lasers extended from its flanks and hung limp like a towing cable. The pod began to spin furiously, whipping the lasers to form a deadly circular saw.

Ishiro smiled.

Yeop, surmised Duke.

The vessel spun at a speed that made it unrecognizable as a spacecraft. It clipped a few nearby scout ships en route to its destination: a Four I's battle cruiser. The diminutive saucer approached the hulking cruiser without so much as a warning shot. As the neon saw made contact with the cruiser's hull, it set off a chain reaction of destruction. The battle cruiser tried to belatedly turn its attention to the tiny invader, but its attacks only damaged itself. Yeop's buzzsaw cut through the outer hull and then the tiny craft disappeared. Moments later, it emerged from the other side of the cruiser, ceased spinning, and jetted away to a patch of clear space. The battle cruiser had been cut in two.

Inside the bunker, the mood was becoming ever more positive. The renewed sense of hope was palpable. The Four I's force still maintained a numbers edge on Maxx, Yeop, and the Earthers, but it was now a much more evenly-matched battle. Neither looked to be able to claim a decisive victory. And that played into the Queen and her followers' plan.

"You know what? You guys are really pissing me off!" shouted Admiral LePaco from the screen.

"Did you patch him in?" the Queen asked Earl.

"I think he's found a way to override our comms," replied the furry bartender.

"Yes, I did," smirked LePaco. "It's not that hard, especially with your operation. So you think you're so smart, and that these savage Earthers are going to take out my forces. It doesn't matter. I came to get the Orb, and get it I will. You're about to feel the full might of Admiral LePaco!"

The admiral's eyes were bulging, his nostrils flaring, and Duke could almost feel the tension of his clenched jaw through the transmission.

"This revolt ends now," the maniacal tyrant declared before ending the transmission.

The ancillary monitors showed several sections of the Four I's force breaking off and heading toward the Keltian surface. The plan was working.

That bastard Gemstarr did it, Duke concluded reluctantly. *Maybe he's not such an ass after all.*

Maxx appeared on the primary view screen seconds after LePaco ended his communication.

"I did it, guys. Maxx Gemstarr always delivers," he

boasted, flashing his trademark smile, soaked in self-satisfaction.

Never mind.

There was an excitement in the bunker. Despite the fact that many of these soldiers wouldn't live to have another drink at Cyborg Joe's, they were all jazzed that their plan had successfully made it to phase two.

"LePaco is likely to provide ground cover with some of his Attack Class Scouts," stated Joe. "We just have to survive this, like we've been doing the entire time. We want him to get those troop transports on the ground. When he does, we'll send out a few of ours around Joe's."

"So he'll think that's the extent of our resistance?" asked the male Keltian.

"Yes. And so he'll concentrate his attack on Joe's," added Lutra.

"Or what's left of Joe's," chimed in Duke. His commentary was ignored.

"Once we engage, then our satellite bunkers will attack from behind the enemy lines," continued the Hilterian ambassador. "When LePaco's troops turn their attention to our surprise squadrons, then our reserves here will make themselves known."

The Hausen-Ra commanders raised their swords in unison.

"Your readiness is not in question" said Lutra, acknowledging the skeletal warriors. "If all goes well, the Gartoshian land force will provide the last bit of offense that we need to win the day."

"And prevent an escape," concluded Queen Joe.

"Yes, Queen. That's the long and short of it, everyone. Any objections?"

The crowd silently nodded affirmation.

"What about if LePaco does turn his ships on the ground forces?" asked the Nova Texan.

Laughter rose around him. The beings around Duke showed disbelief on their faces.

"No, really," Duke added. "What if LePaco—"

"I know he's a crazed maniac, but even the admiral wouldn't turn his guns on his own people."

"If it helped him get the Orb, he would."

The subtle chuckles became hearty belly laughs.

Queen Joe hushed the crowd. "Duke, it's a risk that we're going to have to take." She turned her attention to the greater mass in the bunker. "It is now *our* time. We must continue the efforts of those brave fighters in the sky that gave their lives to give us this chance. Let us all prepare for our final stand. We stand together, Keltian, Hilterian, Hausen-Ra, Psitakki, Sabromm, Neprian, Earther, Gartoshian. Everyone. LePaco's push towards domination ends now."

The group erupted into cheers.

CHAPTER 24

PHASE TWO

A S EXPECTED, LEPACO'S FORCES SWEPT over Oldish Kelt, unleashing an impressive load of explosives. However, as none of the Queen's army was on the surface, the bombing wasn't overly effective—unless you were a tree or a rock or a patch of shrubbery that had managed to survive the last few raids. Then it sucked.

"Their transports are landing," said Earl, his voice crackling through the communication device that Queen Joe held. "Our prognostications are holding true. They should be visible from the front steps of the bar."

"Great, Earl. If things go sideways, I just want to thank you for everything."

The Glyptodian did not respond, but Duke thought he heard a subtle whimper from the device.

It would be quite a sight to see a Glyptodian, seven feet of fur-covered mass, reduced to tears.

"We'll make our way through the bar and then fan out as we exit," commanded Joe. "We want them to notice us. Make yourselves big. Fire pulses into the air. You don't need to even hit anything. Just make them aware of us."

"You mean what's left of the bar," interjected Duke. "I

don't think it's going to give us much cover after all of these attacks."

The Queen did not acknowledge the bounty hunter and proceeded to give orders to the select squad chosen to draw the attention of the Four I's ground force. Queen Joe was included because she could make the biggest scene. Lightning bolts shooting from her fingertips with giant whirly tornadoes surrounding her arms would be a good start to getting noticed. Duke was included for the same reason: he had Ol' Betsy, and she could make a ton of noise. Ishiro'shea joined them because that was what sidekicks did. Duke had loaned him his laser revolver after making a joke to Ishiro about reflecting the sun from his sword to burn the invading enemies like ants. His partner had not seen the humor. Lutra, the Hilterian, and a host of Keltian volunteer soldiers rounded out the squad. Po'l stayed with the forces in the bunker, including the Hausen-Ra, since he was selected to lead that charge. Lilly remained in the base as well, as she was the point of contact to her brethren on the other side of the planet. Gha stayed back because he was so short that he wasn't likely to get noticed by the Four I's soldiers, even if he had a bazooka strapped to his shoulder.

"Now!" shouted Queen Joe. She motioned the group to make its way through the basement of Cyborg Joe's and up to the main level.

They emerged from the cellar to find the bar pretty much intact. Sure, the rogue neon sign had fallen off the wall. There were some broken martini glasses. A few barstools had toppled over. A grease fire or two burned from the kitchen area. But, all in all, it wasn't too far off from a normal night at Cyborg Joe's.

"How... what... how did..." Duke stammered.

The Queen looked back at the confused bounty hunter. "I told you it was made of some pretty stern stuff."

Queen Joe blasted electric charges into the air, lobbing some as far as the transport ships themselves. Duke gave Ol' Betsy the stage and had her belt out a solo that shook the clouds. Lutra, an accomplished sniper—as were most Hilterians—picked off a few unsuspecting Four I's watchmen in the shadows of the largest transport ship. The Keltians screamed. A lot. And it was loud. Louder than the blaster pulses that they fired aimlessly into the air. It was soon apparent that the Four I's forces had noticed the rebels. Troops started to pour out of their ships and head toward the galaxy's loudest bar.

"There has to be fifty thousand of them and counting," commented a Keltian soldier.

"I think more than that," added another.

"Fifty thousand—" began Lutra.

"Or more," interrupted another Keltian.

"Yes, fifty thousand *or more*—to what? A dozen? Those odds aren't the greatest I've encountered," continued the Hilterian.

"But they aren't the worst we've had," added Duke. "Right, Ish?"

The ninja agreed. The Hilterian shook her head.

"Seriously," the bounty hunter continued, "this one time on—what's the name of that planet, Ish?"

His thought was interrupted by an explosion a mere ship's length in front of them.

"Holy hedgehogs, that was close!"

Duke retaliated with a counterblast from Betsy. He wasn't sure if he killed anything at that distance, but he was pretty confident he at least hurt someone.

The Queen stepped to the front of the configuration. Just as she had done before, she became entrenched in a cosmic trance. Clouds of smoky gas consumed her hands. In a flash, she heaved a flurry of electric bolts into the approaching army. She repeated this over and over.

Though successful, it seemed to prompt the forces to pick

up their speed. And it seemed like the stream from the transports was never-ending.

The Four I's sent more long-range projectiles towards the group of rebels. Their aim left something to be desired; the explosions erupted behind Cyborg Joe's.

"Back in the bar, now!" shouted Queen Joe. "Now!"

The group retreated into the confines of the sturdy infrastructure.

Joe grabbed her communications device. "Earl, send them in!"

The sounds of the marching juggernaut were steady, and steadily increasing in volume. But then they stopped. What had been orderly and organized, even amidst the Queen's lightning strikes and blasts from Betsy, became chaotic. This was not like the good folks of Intergalactic Infrastructure Improvement, Incorporated.

They're distracted, thought Duke.

At this realization, he looked at Queen Joe. She returned a wry grin.

"Phase two is on," she said to her team.

Lutra returned from the front steps of Cyborg Joe's.

"They're fully engaged with the troops from the satellite bunkers. Unbelievable. They just assumed that we were the last remaining soldiers," she said.

"Excellent," said Joe. "It's time we make this into a Four I's sandwich."

She raised her communications device. "Earl, tell Po'l that he's up. He can send some up through the basement. The main force can use the back exit, the one the Hausen-Ra used."

"It has been communicated," said the Glyptodian. "Good luck."

"You too, Earl."

Before Earl could sign off, the soldiers flowed from the basement door, through the bar, and out into the skirmish. This squad consisted of Keltians, Sabromms, and Psitakki and were led by the feisty Goother Rat, Gha. Po'l's force, a combined unit of Keltians and Hausen-Ra, was likely exiting through the back of the bunker to meet up with Gha and complete the final clamp on the Four I's contingent. Phase two was in full effect.

"What now?" Duke asked Queen Joe. "What do you want us to do? Join 'em?"

"As much as we'd love to have you out there fighting the Four I's soldiers, I need you, Ishiro'shea, and Lutra to help me get to LePaco. He's here, and we need to either capture him along with the other two artifacts, or kill him."

"You think he's here on the surface?"

"I do. Possibly in the back, near the transports. I have a feeling that he's a let-my-army-clear-me-a-path kinda guy."

"No argument there," replied Duke. "So..."

"So, we blast our way to those transports," she proclaimed.

The Queen's wry grin grew even wryer.

CHAPTER 25

A QUEEN AND HER PORTAL

"HE HAS TO BE SOMEWHERE by those ships," shouted Queen Joe as she sent a group of Four I's infantrymen into the air with an explosive lightning strike. Another subsequent blast cleared an even wider path for the foursome to advance.

"We still have a long way to go," added Lutra. She rattled off three pulses, knocking down three soldiers with her impeccable marksmanship. "I'm just hoping that he's still there when we make it. He could run if he sees the odds are turning."

Duke knelt down and fired Ol' Betsy, giving the invading quartet even more room.

"Thanks, Duke," said Queen Joe. "I don't think he views this battle here as anything that can be 'won' or 'lost.' I think this is just a necessary mechanism to get me out in the open." She paused and whipped a few more deadly bolts into the Four I's forces. "Or at least in a situation where I can be captured. Or more accurately, the Orb."

Ishiro'shea slashed his katana through a pair of well-armed soldiers.

Though their view was narrowly focused on the forces blocking their path to the transport ships, it was apparent that the Queen's strategy to envelop the Four I's army was working. Duke could even hear and see some of the advancing Keltians from the satellite bunkers making their way to the center of the battle. The Hausen-Ra—noted warriors, especially in close-quarters hand-to-hand combat—were simply overwhelming their opponents. This had the makings for a decisive victory.

"I'm afraid you're right, Queen," screamed Duke, in between blasts from Betsy.

"About what?"

"LePaco. He doesn't care about his soldiers and this fight. No more than he cares about ours. But that brings us to a really big issue."

"And what's that?" asked Joe.

"Yeah, what's that?" added Lutra.

"Those."

Approaching from the sky, barely higher than the tallest building in Oldish Kelt—before the recent bombings, that is—was an attack squad. Ten or so Attack Class Scouts dashed over the battlefield and let loose an artillery barrage, spraying a combination of lasers and short-range missiles across both forces. Explosions overwhelmed large expanses of the battlefield. Duke and Ishiro'shea dove to the ground to avoid the long, erratic reach of the shrapnel. Queen Joe ended up on her stomach next to the bounty hunters.

"I can't believe he—" she began, then corrected herself. "No, I can absolutely believe that he would fire on his own men. It's my fault for only expecting rational tactics from him. This is my fault."

Duke wanted to take credit for considering that this was a possibility, but he knew this was not the time. Barely anything is ideal when one is being shot at by an entire attack squad of spaceships. The frequency of the explosions increased. The casualties on both sides were beginning to mount. Duke fired Betsy into the air, hoping to hit something, but judging by the consistent barrage being unleashed from the air, it was clear that he had not.

"Do we have any air support?" yelled Duke through the hysteria. "Can Lilly send in the Gartoshian troops? Maybe they've got some cannons on that transport."

Joe simply flashed her communication device. It was damaged beyond repair.

Shit.

"We need to do *something*," shouted Lutra. "We can't survive this much longer."

The Queen clambered to her feet. Once again, she entered her trance. The air began to whirl around her, smoke clouding up around her hands. She raised her right hand and flung a series of bolts into the air. One clipped a ship and sent it hurtling into the Keltian soil, where it erupted into a huge fireball. She sent another wave out, knocking out another two ships. The remaining ships in the fleet peeled off and reengaged, focusing their firepower squarely on Queen Joe.

The inter-dimensional bar owner crouched down as the fighters approached, turning her back to the aircraft. A velvet bag hung from her right hip, barely noticeable. In the hectic fury of war, these details are often overlooked, even by the keenest observer. Duke hadn't noticed it until now. But, as the most powerful single entity that he had come across in his many travels turned her back to an airborne onslaught, that's all he *could* notice. Queen Joe reached into the bag and pulled something. She held aloft a glowing violet sphere. The Orb.

The smoky gas that engulfed her ceased. All that remained were the Queen and her Orb. She thrust the sphere in the direction of the attacking ships. Violet beams emerged from the mysterious artifact and fanned out across the Keltian sky. Four of the ships disintegrated immediately. The remaining three circled and regrouped.

The Four I's vessels surrounded Queen Joe and closed in, their pulses targeted squarely on her. The Orb sent out what looked like twisted vines, electrified and radiating bright purple. The vines absorbed the entire round of laser blasts from the Four I's aircraft, knocking out two of the ships in a beautiful explosion. The surviving vessel swooped away, presumably in order to rejoin the much more predictable battle in space.

The ground forces on both sides were all stunned. They did not resume hand-to-hand warfare. Now both sides understood that they were targets of LePaco's assault.

I'm sure they're questioning what side they're on, thought Duke.

"So did we win?" asked a Keltian soldier who had tried to find cover from the attack near Duke and Ishiro'shea. "Did she just win the war?"

Duke started to answer but was distracted. LePaco clearly didn't think anything was over.

Casting a shadow over the entire area around Cyborg Joe's was a fully-equipped battle cruiser. *More* than fully-equipped.

"Holy hedgehogs, they spared no expense on this one. I've seen Titans with less firepower," remarked Duke.

Queen Joe said nothing. She held the Orb in both hands, above her head.

"Concentrate your fire on that ship," ordered Lutra. "Now!"

All rebel soldiers within earshot did as she instructed. Duke rattled off a few puffs of anger from Betsy. The effect of the ground force attack was the equivalent of an ant biting a Mega-Troll. The enhanced battle cruiser pressed on.

The first volley from the advancing ship ripped a crater in the ground, directly in front of the Queen. Soldiers on both sides scattered.

"If that thing hits her, she's dead. The Orb will be destroyed," screamed Lutra. "We have to do something!"

Duke looked at Ishiro'shea quizzically.

He's as empty on ideas as I am, he concluded.

"We played right into his hands, didn't we?" Lutra continued, clearly panicked. "He *wanted* us out here."

"It appears so. LePaco knew we would look for him—and it left us exposed," added the bounty hunter. "Damn."

As the battle cruiser readied another attack, Queen Joe remained motionless, almost tranquil. Her response to LePaco's plan was anything but. The Orb pulsed and shook, now glowing an even brighter shade of purple. Not a single bolt left the spheroid, however. It just vibrated, rose a few inches above her skyward facing palms... then it began to spin. And spin. It spun so fast that it was almost unrecognizable as an orb.

The sky to the right of the battle cruiser sparked, the sparks became a crimson crackle, and that turned into an untamed portal. It looked like the astral anomaly that had sent the *Deus Ex Machina* to Neprius, albeit smaller and less stable. As it formed, it leapt out like an eel emerging from a cave in the sea floor, and consumed the entire front half of the cruiser. It disappeared just as quickly, leaving an inoperable back half of a spacecraft floating uncertainly for a moment in the Keltian sky. Then the posterior of the ship crashed to the ground, just beyond the battlefield.

Everybody around the bar erupted in cheers, rebels and Four I's soldiers alike. LePaco's latest ploy was officially foiled.

Queen Joe did not move. The Orb remained slightly above her outstretched hands, still spinning at an unbelievable rate. The unstable portal reappeared above the battlefield. The Queen was locked in a catatonic state, a symbiotic relationship with the magic rock.

"She's doing it without any mustangsen," Duke said to Ishiro'shea. The ninja looked to be as shocked as the Nova Texan. "How's she doing that?"

"And why hasn't she stopped?" Lutra chimed in.

"There must be something else on its way," responded Duke. "Another wave of attacks. She has to sense *something*."

"I would think that they have all they can handle with

Maxx, the Earthers, and the Gartoshians," said the Hilterian. "LePaco had a huge fleet but it wasn't infinite."

Cutting through an innocent patch of drifting clouds and heading directly for the entranced Queen Joe was a sleek salmon-colored spaceship. Its license plate read "Mister Macho."

CHAPTER 26

A QUEEN AND HER EVEN
BIGGER PORTAL

DUKE HAD ONLY SEEN LEPACO'S ship from a distance, and at that moment, it had been escaping the fiery remains of an Armada Titan. He hadn't studied it, analyzed it, or even paid that close of attention. Now it was staring down directly at him. And it was an impressive specimen, color scheme and vanity plate notwithstanding. The bounty hunter had never seen anything like it.

Queen Joe's hands dropped to her sides, while the Orb still hovered above her. She flung both hands towards LePaco's ship and rays of electric violence beamed outward from her fingers. The Orb let loose a third bolt. All three struck the forward bow of the ship. It was a crippling blast. The explosion was immense. But LePaco's ship pressed on, unfazed by the strike. In fact, there was almost no visible damage. The Queen repeated her gesture, rocking the ship but not hurting it. LePaco countered with a three-hundred-and-sixty-degree expulsion of bombs, missiles, and lasers. His spray-and-pray tactic took out everything in its path. Those unharmed fled. The Queen, backed by Duke, Ishiro'shea, and Lutra, remained, facing off in a showdown with the awesome ship.

The Orb slowly descended into Joe's hands. The astral

anomaly that had been floating harmlessly in the sky was suddenly awake, activated by the Queen. It lunged in the same manner as when it had destroyed the battle cruiser—but LePaco dodged it. Though still in her trance, the Queen flinched in dismay at the miss. It leapt again. Another miss.

"It doesn't even look like he's trying that hard," said Duke aloud. "Is LePaco that good of a pilot?"

A third miss by the rogue portal. The Queen's twitches were becoming more frequent and more intense.

The portal vanished with a puff and then appeared above the Queen's position, level with the admiral's craft. The crimson glow from the astral anomaly cast a shadow over the entire battlefield; the thing seemed to have doubled in size. The portal crackled and hissed but emitted no heat, and it produced no wind. It was just colored noise.

Queen Joe convulsed. The contortions would have broken the bones of most humanoids, but the Queen appeared to feel nothing. The harder she jerked, the bigger the portal grew. Admiral LePaco's ship did not fire on the portal or at Queen Joe.

What's he up to? thought Duke.

As the portal expanded to the point where its outer rim almost reached the ground, a hatch on the forward bow of LePaco's ship opened. The barrel of a cannon extended out, aimed directly at the portal.

"What's he going to do with that?" Duke said to Ishiro'shea and Lutra, pointing at the gun. "Something that size won't do much damage to a fragile egg, let alone a pissed-off inter-dimensional being with an unhinged portal."

"An unhinged portal that has already taken out a battle cruiser," added the Hilterian.

"Exactly."

The portal's growth spurt finally halted. The Queen's movement came to a stop as well.

Nothing can survive this, Duke thought. *Is this going to be it? The end?*

LePaco's insignificant-looking cannon spat out what appeared to be a pretty insignificant-looking silver beam. The velocity of the beam was just as uninspiring, moving towards the astral anomaly at the pace of a Daedean beach snail.

The portal let out an ear-piercing shriek and rushed towards the ship.

It struck the pedestrian ray and then stopped. The portal began to shake and pulse and then dispersed into billions of particles, splattering a red dust over the Keltian landscape.

"What just happened?" asked an astounded Duke LaGrange, addressing no one in particular. "Did that gun just neutralize the Orb's portals? How...?"

Ishiro'shea tugged on Duke's arm, jolting his attention from the free-falling crimson clouds of portal dust. The ninja raced past even as Duke was still collecting his thoughts as to what just happened. The emerald-clad martial artist hustled to where the Queen had been. She was no longer standing or in her trance; she was sprawled out on the grass, motionless. The bounty hunter and Lutra made their way to her.

"Is she breathing?" asked Lutra. Ishiro'shea nodded. "Good. What was that thing?"

"I have no idea but it totally knocked out the portal," said Duke. "We have to get her back inside."

Ishiro'shea began to lift the Queen to her feet.

"The Key," she mumbled. "He's got the Key."

"What, Queen? What are you saying?" asked Duke.

She cleared her throat.

"LePaco's figured out how to use the Key on its own. That blast was from the Amplification Key... the Key."

"He's learned how to harness it? Already? But, even if he did capture Ish's parents, he's only had it briefly. How did he figure it out so quickly?"

Ishiro'shea squeezed Duke's shoulder. His eyes said everything.

"Your parents told him?" said Duke. "No. I don't believe it."

"I'm sure they were tortured or tricked," suggested Lutra.

The Queen nodded in agreement.

"Well, how would *they* know?"

The ninja lowered his head. He squeezed Duke's shoulder again and pointed to his own heart. It took Duke a second to realize what his partner was trying to say.

He doesn't mean "me." Heart. The Heart of Nobunaga.

Duke's brain continued to race.

"From the accounts—the legends—of Takeo Nobunaga?" Duke guessed.

Ishiro'shea nodded.

"Yes," the injured Queen said faintly.

"I bet that's why she tore up the master's office, not from a scuffle but looking for any of the actual records," added Duke.

"That's great and all, but we gotta go, guys," commanded Lutra. "As in *now*."

LePaco's ship had landed upon the open plain. Troops and special guards poured out of the vessel and surrounded the ship.

"He's in there," Joe added, now on her feet, leaning for support on Duke. "We have to get him."

"Not like this," Duke added. "Plus, they don't have enough to get through our ground forces, especially without the help of the Four I's ground soldiers. LePaco royally screwed that partnership up."

"Duke," began Lutra in a voice that didn't inspire much confidence, "I think you underestimated his plan to get to us."

The admiral's ship began to transform. Compartments pulled apart to reveal hidden artillery units. Paneling disappeared, and even more weapons emerged. What was once a sleek deep-space fighting vessel was now a stationary war machine with enough firepower to take out a mid-sized moon.

The battle station unleashed a raging fury equal to a thousand rounds from Ol' Betsy. Single blasts toppled buildings. The explosions of light and sound made the chaos even more challenging to navigate.

"Order a retreat," pleaded Joe to Duke and Lutra. "Please."

With no working communication device, the rebels were left with only their voices. And, for once, Duke's voice was wholly inadequate.

The few within a tight enough radius to hear fled for the cover of the bar. But the legions of Keltians and Hausen-Ra followed their original orders honorably. They regrouped and charged at the impenetrable fortress of death.

"They're all going to die," cried the Queen. "LePaco is going to slaughter them. That thing is going to slaughter them."

Another round of chaotic devastation fell upon those in the battlefield.

"We have to go now," shouted Lutra.

"I agree," replied Duke. He hoisted the Queen onto his shoulder. The quartet began to retreat to Cyborg Joe's.

"No, we have to help them," the Queen moaned from atop the bounty hunter.

"LePaco's special guard is on the move. This last spray caused enough confusion that they have a direct path to us and to the bar," screamed Lutra as she attempted to cover their escape with erratic blasts from her sniper rifle. "They'll be on top of us soon. We have to pick it up."

Duke accelerated to a sprint; at least, the best he could do with a passenger aboard.

"We need more cover," screamed the Hilterian.

"Our entire army needs cover from that thing," yelled the bounty hunter.

Rising above the top of Cyborg Joe's was an image that Duke and Ishiro'shea instantly recognized. It was home. It was the *Deus*.

"I thought we lost her," Duke said to Ishiro'shea, only slowing his pace slightly to examine his captainless ship.

But on closer examination he saw that it wasn't captainless at all. Even at that distance, he recognized the tiny silhouette standing next to one of the side windows at the bow of the ship. Po'l.

The *Deus* wobbled a bit.

Easy there. Be gentle to her.

The ship stabilized and then darted towards LePaco's military installation. It wasn't alone. A gargantuan Gartoshian troop transport accompanied by a handful of Gartoshian Fighter ships serving as its escort fanned out behind the *Deus*.

"We have our cover," Duke said, gaining confidence. "Not sure how long it'll last, but if I know my ship, it'll be enough to get us to safety and then some. And, hopefully, it'll give our friends a chance to take out that thing."

"Maybe," said Lutra doubtfully. "Maybe it will. But we'll still have to deal with the admiral and his officers. They're through the line and closing ground."

The foursome pulled themselves up the steps in front of Cyborg Joe's. Lutra rattled off a few shots. Ishiro'shea did the same with Duke's pulse pistol.

"I'll take Joe down to the bunker," said Duke. "You two hide out in the bar and try to hold the admiral at bay."

"Not much of a plan," said Lutra.

"I'm not the best with plans. I'm more of a 'wing it' type of guy."

"Just do it," snapped Queen Joe, still hanging from Duke's shoulder. "As long as we have the Orb and it's shielded from that cannon, we have a chance. I'll bet that he hasn't mastered the use of either the Shield or the Key without filtering it through his machinery."

"That's a chance we're going to have to take," concluded Duke.

LePaco's special force was in sight now, closing in on Cyborg Joe's. There was no doubt that hidden within that throng of soldiers was Admiral LePaco and, possibly, Mazilda Cloax.

CHAPTER 27

I GAVE YOU THAT KNIFE

ISHIRO'SHEA AND LUTRA ZIPPED BY Duke and into Cyborg Joe's. Duke, still carrying the injured Queen Joe, was gasping for air as he approached the threshold of the popular drinking establishment and temporary headquarters for the ragtag resistance against Admiral LePaco. The Queen wasn't heavy, and he had no shortage of adrenaline considering the circumstances, but he was wearing down. Luckily, safety lay just beyond that swinging door.

In the back of the bar, Duke noticed a friendly face, surrounded by a handful of other friendly faces. Lilly, armed with some sort of Keltian firearm, was flanked by a dozen or so Keltian soldiers and a pair of Hausen-Ra commanders. They all stood behind a makeshift barrier, prepared for one last stand, if need be. And the need *was* be.

Thank the deity of the week! Duke thought. *Lilly! We have a chance.*

The bounty hunter barely had one boot inside Cyborg Joe's when he felt a stinging pain north of his right hamstring.

I better have not just been shot in the ass, surmised Duke.

The pain sharpened. Then it spread down past his hamstring and into the back of his kneecap. His jog turned into a limp. His limp turned into a tumble. Duke hit the hard floor with a thud, dropping the Queen with an equally cringe-worthy crash.

The bounty hunter looked down through squinted eyes and saw not a mark left by a blaster or rifle, but the pewter hilt of a knife. A throwing dagger, to be exact. Mazilda Cloax's throwing dagger, to be super-duper exact. Luckily for Duke, he recognized this particular dagger, which was one of her shorter blades. If she had connected with one of her favorite throwing daggers, its other end would have ripped through his pelvis and added an extra hole in his belt. But even though it wasn't the most intimidating knife, it hurt. A lot. It was still, after all, a knife that was jabbed into his outer thigh, between his buttock and hip bone.

He looked up and saw Queen Joe struggling to make her way to her feet. He was pleased to see that, at first glance, she appeared to have no knives sticking out of her, and no gunshot wounds.

"Get her! Get Joe!" shouted Duke at Ishiro'shea and Lutra. "Get her behind that wall!"

The pair sprinted to Joe and hoisted her up.

"What about you?" asked the Hilterian.

"I'll be fine. You two take the Queen before she gets shot by these bastards."

Ishiro'shea noticed the dagger. Duke could tell that his partner recognized it immediately.

"Go, Ish. We're all dead if they get her and the Orb. I'll be crawling right behind y'all."

The ninja nodded.

That's why he was Salutatorian.

The sound of the Four I's soldiers' boots rattled the decor in the bar. They were moments away from bull rushing Cyborg Joe's. This was the proverbial "it." Queen Joe's valiant patchwork force would either stop the well-armed Admiral LePaco and his fine-tuned soldiers and save the universe, or else LePaco was about to acquire the final piece in his megalo-maniacal puzzle of conquest. And it was going to happen at Cyborg Joe's.

Duke turned onto his side so that he faced the door, resting his weight on the buttock that wasn't impaled by a dagger. He aimed Betsy at the opening.

"Stay back, everyone," he yelled. "I'm going to take out as many as I can. If they walk through that door, Betsy's greeting 'em with her own interpretation of a handshake."

"I'm coming to get you," shouted Lutra over the increasing volume of the invaders. "Just stay there."

"No, stay back. Queen, tell her to stay back."

The bounty hunter didn't look back to see if the Queen held her back or to say a final goodbye to his long-time companion.

Sorry, Ish. Let me be the hero this time.

"Just make sure to keep that Orb away from LePaco, at all costs," yelled Duke as he aimed Betsy at the entrance.

I hope LePaco has the guts to come through first.

"I don't have the Orb. It's gone. Duke, it's gone!"

It was rare to see Queen Joe actually panicking.

Duke lowered Betsy and quickly scanned the ground around him. Splintered tables. Upturned chars. Shattered neon signs. Puddles of booze. Puddles of other stuff that were likely to never be identified properly.

Along the perimeter wall were a handful of half-circle dining booths. Many a MechaBurger 8000 had been consumed in those seats. Many a culinary adventurer had made their final adventure in those seats as well. The first booth was twice the size of the others, as it was reserved for the plus-sized species of traveler. It was also a favorite of those that preferred to walk on four legs, or six. It was spacious. And a glowing purple sphere rested in the shadows beneath its over-sized table.

The Orb must have fallen when Duke dropped the

Queen. Not only was he the closest to it by a good margin, he was responsible for its current whereabouts.

"I got it," Duke shouted to his cohorts behind the barricade.

The bounty hunter made it onto his knees, balancing his weight on his two hands and one good leg. He pushed off, propelling himself as close to the booth as he could muster. But he was still short. He made his way up again into a similar position.

The sound of the Four I's boots had ceased. In its place was the sound of their guns. They were inside Cyborg Joe's and, as of yet, the Orb was not safe. Duke readied himself for one last lunge. Once he had it, it would be up to his friends to give him enough cover to get back. Or he'd just throw the Orb as far as he could towards them and hope for a miracle. In typical Duke LaGrange fashion, he'd just wing it.

The bounty hunter balanced himself. The firefight had clearly begun, but he could tell by the sound that it was focused around the entrance area.

His jaw cracked. His body hit the floor again. And so did his face.

He turned over to see his worst nightmare; the slightly jaundiced profile of his former love, Mazilda Cloax.

"You punched me," said Duke involuntarily.

"Yeah, and I stabbed you," Cloax added. "How can you be shocked by this?"

"Sorry, habit. I'm used to you being, you know, not a bitch."

Mazilda caught sight of the Orb. She smiled.

Her gaze returned to the Nova Texan. "This time, I am truly sorry, Duke. I never thought I'd be able to kill you but you've forced my hand."

"I wish I could've done something back then that would've prevented you from turning into this."

She unsheathed a blade. The dagger's hilt was pewter,

inlaid with sparkling red jewels; it was an old knife, but it was meticulously preserved by a true master craftsman. Mazilda was a true master.

"I'm sorry—" she began.

"You can't kill me with that knife," interrupted Duke, "I *gave* you that knife."

She paused and looked at the dagger. "So you did."

As she refocused on the bounty hunter, Duke let loose a primal scream as he ripped the throwing dagger from his backside and slashed Mazilda's forearm. It was little more than a superficial cut, but the assassin dropped her blade. Duke took advantage of her being temporarily stunned, and placed a boot into her stomach, causing her to roll back a few paces from where he lay bleeding on the floor. He scurried backwards, propelled by his three good limbs, to the diner booth.

Mazilda recovered and pounced again. Her knee caught his ribcage flush. A backhanded swipe of her hand hit the bounty hunter's jaw with a thud. She hoisted her dagger in the air, but Duke grabbed her arm, preventing it from crashing down on his skull. He held her wrist with his other hand.

Even when Duke was at full strength and not recovering from a knife wound, Mazilda was the much more accomplished fighter. Though he was physically larger, she was stronger, more athletic. But he scored higher than her when it came to the most important aspect of combat, especially when it's of the mortal variety—somehow he always figured out a way to survive. Whether it was an attack of a three-headed ice wombat, having spears hurled at him from a legion of priest warriors, or fighting in a pit fighting tournament on Psitakki, Duke LaGrange found a way.

He knew he couldn't hold Mazilda at bay for much longer, especially as blood continued to flow from his thigh. Mazilda seemed content on staying the course, knowing that she would eventually overpower the bounty hunter.

"You taught me this one," Duke said through clenched teeth.

He let go of her left wrist; the momentum pulled her body downwards. The trajectory of her upper torso led to a collision between Mazilda's face and Duke's fist. The jab struck her across the bridge of the nose. She rolled to the left until she was completely off of Duke, freeing the bounty hunter to retrieve the Orb.

As the firefight intensified, Duke scrambled to the booth and secured the Orb. Aside from stray blasts and ricochets, the shootout had not made its way to the perimeter. It was a straight shot to safety.

With an earsplitting crack the table shattered into two pieces. Duke clung to the Orb, still not on his feet and still sitting in a pool of his own blood.

Standing over him was Mazilda Cloax, nose crooked and bruising. She did not have her trademark dagger aimed at her former partner. Apparently she was done with daggers. Duke was now staring directly into the barrel of a pulse pistol.

He gripped the Orb tighter.

"I could really use some help right now," he said, his eyes darting to the tattered barrier being bombarded by enemy fire. He didn't see Ishiro'shea or Lilly or Lutra or Queen Joe. But he knew they were behind there somewhere.

"I said I could really use some help right now," he shouted at the top of his lungs.

"You're not getting any help today, my love."

Mazilda squeezed the trigger.

CHAPTER 28

INTER-DIMENSIONAL DOOMSDAY DEVICE

DUKE CLOSED HIS EYES, BRACING himself for a quick descent into lifelessness. There was no way that Mazilda Cloax could miss a point-blank shot.

But she did.

The bounty hunter could feel the heat of the ray above his left shoulder; it warmed his neck and crept down his spine. His grip on the Orb remained firm. He slowly opened his eyes. Mazilda was there, a bewildered expression on her face. She was backlit by a roaring red glow.

"What the—" She turned to face the crackling crimson blob.

Out from the portal stepped a muscular, athletic female with unblemished skin a shade somewhere between bronze and orange. She was taller and leaner than the assassin. In her hand was a golden ceremonial staff that had likely been a gift from a certain Neprian priest.

Duke's eyes widened and his jaw hung open. He looked down at the mustangsen pendant that lay against his chest.

Ja'a.

"Who are you?" screeched Mazilda. Her gun was still

pointed at Duke but her attention was now firmly on the rogue portal opening.

The Neprian glanced at Mazilda, then at Duke, and finally, her eyes landed on the gun being pointed at her friend.

"Who are you?" Mazilda shouted again. She turned to face Duke. "Do you know this woman?"

The strike with the staff was sudden and violent. Mazilda crashed to the bar floor and slid near Duke and the Orb. Her gun flew halfway across the room and landed in the middle of the firefight.

"Are you alright?" Ja'a asked, her eyes darting around as she took in the scene of carnage. "What's going on?"

"I'm fine," Duke lied. "But we need to get over there." He pointed towards the barricade. "We need to get *this* over there."

"The Orb? What's it doing—"

"No time, I'll fill you in later. Let's just say that if those guys over there get it, we're all dead."

Ja'a nodded and helped the bleeding bounty hunter to his feet.

"I don't remember you being this heavy," Ja'a joked as they made their way along the perimeter wall, trying not to attract the Four I's attention or gunfire. "I see you need someone to keep you in shape."

"I'll admit, I haven't had to walk across an entire country in search of a magic rock lately," he said through a grimace.

"But it was good exercise," she replied. "And good times."

Duke couldn't see from his wounded position, but he wanted to believe that Ja'a said that with her magnificent smile.

"Who was that with the gun?"

"An old friend."

"Friend?"

"She *was* an old friend," Duke corrected himself.

"What did I tell you about your particular brand of exploits? I know I'm from a 'backwoods rock' as you like to say, but my assumption is that treating people in the manner *you* treat them is universally unacceptable. You were bound to get in trouble."

"This is not one of those cases. By the way, you're in a good mood for someone that's been deposited in the middle of a war," Duke remarked.

"Let's just say it's good to see you again."

"I'm really glad to see you too. And not just because you saved my ass."

"Looks like I was a bit late on that front," Ja'a commented, playfully patting the bounty hunter's bloodstained hip.

He yelped. "Ouch!"

"Sorry, I didn't—"

Duke felt a force as powerful as a Trampling Death Robots drum solo hit his lower back. The jolt launched him shoulder-first into the wall. He crumpled to the floor. He sighed internally. *Not the floor again.*

Mazilda Cloax leapt to her feet, having tackled the bounty hunter. Ja'a's stumble from the unexpected attack had separated her from Duke and had allowed Mazilda to situate herself between them. The assassin drew her favorite dagger. Ja'a countered with Vernglet Wip's ceremonial rod.

Ja'a blocked Mazilda's first charge, redirecting her out of striking distance. Cloax lunged but, once again, Ja'a was too quick, landing a sharp jab into Mazilda's abdomen with the butt of the staff. Mazilda grimaced but remained focused on the Neprian. Another approach, another denial. Mazilda's face changed from its jaundiced hue to a red equal to that of the portal that brought her opponent here. The struggle raged; Mazilda's anger-fueled advances were all thwarted but Ja'a's fluid combinations with her staff also never found the mark. It was a battle of equals.

A stray blast from one of the Four I's soldiers struck the floor in front of Ja'a, sending fragments into the air and into the face of the Neprian. She closed her eyes and turned her head to avoid the debris.

Mazilda pounced with her dagger aimed at the distracted warrior. Ja'a dodged the death blow with a quick slide to the right, whipped her body around in a full circle, her back now towards her devious counterpart. The momentum of her spin propelled her staff with even more velocity; when it struck Mazilda, she fell to the floor with a noise louder than the laser strike.

"Get the Orb and go, Duke," barked the still dazed Ja'a.

The bounty hunter pulled himself up, leaning on the wall for support. The Orb was tucked away in the crook of one arm and his other braced against the wall. His hobble grew even more pronounced. But the finish line was in sight.

The dagger embedded itself into the wall an eyelash's length from his face. Duke recoiled with shock, causing him to lose his balance; he caught himself with his right arm before he crashed into the floor yet again. The Orb pried itself loose from his right arm as he hit the ground. Oddly, it didn't bounce: when it connected with the floor, it stopped immediately as if it had been lobbed into a pile of thick sludge. Then, despite having no visible means of locomotion, it began to roll slowly away from Duke. He made one last effort to swipe at it, but it was already out of reach.

He looked up to see the wounded Mazilda. She locked eyes with her former lover and smiled. For the first time, Duke saw her for who she was, or rather who she had become. It shouldn't have taken him this long, considering the atrocities that she had caused, or stood by and let happen, but for the first time, Duke realized that she was evil. *Very* evil. Admiral LePaco-level evil.

Mazilda's smile lasted only a moment. Ja'a's staff struck her head with a focused force.

If she isn't dead, at the very least she's not going anywhere for a while, thought Duke.

Now Ja'a seemed to notice the rolling Orb. *It wasn't the first time that she'd seen this particular Orb behave this way,* remembered Duke.

"I'll get it," she shouted.

The Orb continued its path; it was directly in the center of the ongoing firefight between the rebel holdouts behind the barricade and the Four I's soldiers.

"No!" Duke screamed with as much power as he could muster. "You'll get shot before you're anywhere near it."

She furled her brow. "I can get it."

"Don't," pleaded the Nova Texan.

He realized that the matrix of lasers and plasma blasts that had crisscrossed the bar had now stopped. Both sides had noticed the glowing violet sphere. It had slowed to a stop and was now nestled comfortably on a shattered floor plank.

"I really can get it now," said the Neprian. She turned to retrieve the Orb, then stopped. Her next steps were backwards towards Duke, not in the direction of the inter-dimensional artifact.

Admiral Lothario LePaco emerged from behind the Four I's lines. He wore his usual garish ensemble, but on his left forearm was draped a shield. *The* Shield. The grand prize of the Tournament of the Shield of the Colossal Calamari. One third of a weapon that could tear apart the fabric of a universe with the nonchalance of somebody brushing their teeth. Furthermore, hanging around his neck was an exceptionally shiny piece of jeweled wire, attached to which was an equally shiny locket. The Amplification Key.

LePaco was followed by a single Four I's commander. He had to be important because he had a lot of medals.

No one fired at either of them. Though the Shield that LePaco carried was one of the most powerful objects in the whole of the universe, his human shield was just as effective. Pressed against him, hands bound behind her back, was Ishiro'shea's mother. The Four I's commander tugged on the chains that held the Father, Ishiro'shea's dad, in check, despite his struggles.

"Shoot him!" boomed the Father. "Forget about us! Shoot him! Now!"

No one fired.

LePaco threw Yumi Nobunaga-Flaherty to the ground. He raised his shielded arm. As the Orb sped towards him, the rebel forces stood motionless in shock. Even Ishiro'shea remained inert.

"Shoot him," echoed Duke. "Now!"

LePaco picked up the Orb. His cackle filled every nook and crevice in Cyborg Joe's.

"You morons," he said, his voice coated in condescension. He held the Orb in the air and examined it.

The recovering Queen Joe peered over the barricade. Duke could see the horror in her eyes.

"Fire! Fire! With everything you've got," she commanded.

The rebels opened fire. Duke scanned the crowd. He didn't see Ishiro'shea.

LePaco lifted his left arm, raising the Shield against the attack. It emitted a blinding light along with a shockwave that sent everyone back a few paces. Duke noted that it wasn't overly painful, more confusing, since light typically didn't move objects. It did provide a distraction, though. He and Ja'a were able to sneak behind the barricade to their allies without being noticed.

The illumination dimmed as the light appeared to be sucked back into the Shield.

Both forces looked around in disbelief. Not a single blast had made its way through. The Four I's were unharmed. As were Ishiro'shea's parents.

Admiral LePaco's cackle escalated in volume and intensity. He rotated his arm so that the Shield faced the ceiling. He slammed down the Orb in the direct center of the Shield. The sound it made was indescribable—it was at once a deep drumming beat and a high-pitched whine; a skull-crushing intensity married with a delicate purr. And yet it wasn't at all any of those things. It was simply indescribable. And it didn't let up. The Orb remained in a stationary position, defying the laws of physics by not rolling off the sloping face of the Shield.

LePaco then yanked the Key from the necklace and jabbed it into the solid Orb. Somehow, the Key cut through its surface like a plastic spork into a tub of never-ending mayonnaise. The noise reached an agonizing climax... then vanished. Silence consumed Cyborg Joe's for the first time in its existence.

The trio of inter-dimensional artifacts had now become a single inter-dimensional doomsday device.

And, despite the efforts of Queen Joe, Duke LaGrange, Ishiro'shea, and countless other brave souls, it was in the hands of Admiral Lothario LePaco.

The universe's days were now numbered.

CHAPTER 29

NINETY-NINE

THE NEWLY-FORMED INSTRUMENT OF UNFATHOMABLE destruction glowed upon Admiral LePaco's forearm. The uplighting effect added an extra layer of creepiness to his facial expression. Though Duke believed the Queen regarding the power of this weapon, it was hard not to find it outlandish, looking like the cosmic ray guns in the children's books that his adopted mother would read to him. After all, it was a glowing metallic pendant sticking out of a glowing purple bowling ball adhered, somehow, to a rickety and old glowing shield—like the cherry on top of a scoop of ice cream. And all of this was strapped to the forearm of an outlandishly-dressed super villain. Had the very existence of the universe not depended on the next few moments, there would probably have been comic absurdity to be found in the situation. Then again, what *is* the universe if not comically absurd?

Who had money on the universe ending like this? Duke thought.

The injured Queen Joe raised an eyebrow at the bounty hunter. "You know, Duke," she said, struggling through the pain, "I always knew that you'd be part of the end of the universe."

Duke didn't reply. He just shrugged his shoulders.

A shot was fired from behind the rebels' barricade. It missed LePaco and took out a Four I's infantryman. The admiral looked up and sneered. He thrust his forearm and the unique apparatus attached to it towards the rebel line. A blinding light followed by a shockwave. But LePaco looked displeased.

He wanted to obliterate everyone. That bastard's just winging this, realized Duke. *I can't be out-winged by this dude.*

The admiral repeated the gesture. The same result. A third time, same thing. In frustration, LePaco slapped the Shield. The disc began to twirl; the Orb and the Key levitated a few inches above the Shield as it picked up velocity.

This can't be good, thought Duke.

"Should we shoot it?" barked Lilly. "Queen, what should we do?"

Joe waved her off groggily. "No, we can't harm it. We just have to hope that LePaco hasn't figured out how to use it properly."

The spinning Shield began to hiss and wail. Bulbous droplets of light began to peel off of the whirling disc and scatter across the floor of Cyborg Joe's.

"What's going on, Queen?" asked Duke. "Tell me this is normal and you know what's happening."

All eyes focused on Joe as she replied, "I'm afraid I'm not quite sure. But LePaco seems just as confused."

Abruptly, the spinning stopped. The Orb and Key returned to their stationary positions atop the Shield. The light droplets remained dispersed across the ground as motionless puddles of golden illumination. They were quite beautiful.

The pools of light began to expand, their diameters doubling, then tripling. The light then began to flow upwards, each puddle becoming a different height. The glow intensified, then vanished.

Standing where each of the droplets had landed were numerous beings. No two of them were the same. Some were humanoid. Some were reptiloid. There were a few with wings. More than a few more with horns. One looked like he was made out of molten lava. Another looked like he was made out of notebook paper. Duke swore he saw one that was a pumpkin with fangs and a machete. An eclectic menagerie of alien species with one thing in common—they all appeared to be readying for combat.

"There have to be hundreds of them," a Keltian commented. "Who are they?"

"Do we shoot *them*?" asked Lilly.

"There aren't hundreds of them," replied Joe. "There are ninety-nine."

"Nice party trick, Queen," remarked Duke. "But I don't think the exact number really matters right now. The fact is that there's a lot more of them than us. And they're fully armed."

Ja'a squeezed Duke's wrist.

"Fine, I'll shut up now," he whispered in response.

"It *does* matter, Duke. There's ninety-nine because these are the previous winners of the Tournament of the Shield."

"Wait, what?"

"Apparently, the Shield summoned them."

"How? Some of those dudes have to be a million cycles old."

"Watch it with the ageism," shot back Joe. "I passed that mark a long time ago."

"Sorry."

"I think I know what happened," said the Queen.

"What's the Tournament of the Shield?" asked Ja'a.

"A story for another time," replied Duke.

"When the artifacts were built," began Joe, "the Shield

was the only one constructed with a fail-safe in case of abuse. The others should've been; it was a really poor oversight. If a single being stayed in contact with the Shield for an extended period of time, the assumption was that the being in question probably wasn't using it for good. I'm not sure how that time translated to this dimension but my guess is many cycles. Then it would sort of, well, self-implode."

"What does that even mean?" inquired the bounty hunter.

"I'm not entirely sure about that, but I think it would take the abuser and suck them into an inter-dimensional pocket of existence. A purgatory of sorts. After that, I don't know."

"And each of these chumps kept that trophy close by until it gobbled them up, I suppose. Between their press tours, photo ops, and so on and so forth. It probably was a big part of their post-tournament lives."

"That does make sense," said the Queen in between winces.

The newly-appeared collection of beings looked as confused as the rebels. The admiral ordered his men back, some exiting the crowded bar. His eyes were wide and the corners of his mouth reached his ears. He let loose an uncontrolled laugh, teetering on the brink of hysteria.

"Lost warriors of the Shield," the admiral proclaimed, "I am your Shield Master. I have given you all a second chance."

The ninety-nine former champions all turned to face LePaco.

"Unfortunately, it looks like LePaco also figured out who they were," commented Duke.

The admiral continued, "You have waited a long time to return to this universe—"

One of the beings, a gargantuan six-armed combatant, cut him off. "You're telling me, brother," he groaned. "Have you ever been stuck on an island for five hundred thousand cycles without aging?"

"What species is that guy?" Duke asked the Queen in a low voice.

"I think he's a Timorian. Ancient race. They died out thousands of cycles ago. I've only met a few but they've all been pretty good folks."

"I have not, my friend," said the admiral to the horned Timorian. "But you are back now. You and your fellow champions have been brought back to help me rid this planet of these insolent bastards that stand before you."

The former champions didn't rush towards the rebel line. They just stood there. Most just whispered amongst themselves.

"And why should we do that?" said another combatant, who stepped forward to stand mere paces from the admiral and the Shield. He was Psitakki.

"Ah, you must be Grozzel. Grozzel the Great, if I remember correctly."

"Just Grozzel," the Psitakki replied.

"Then as the first champion of the Tournament, you must know that your horde is under my control, as I have the last remaining holy Shield. It is your destiny to do my bidding."

The Psitakki looked back at his colleagues and rolled his eyes, then turned his attention back to LePaco. "I don't think it works that way. At least, I've never heard that. I definitely didn't sign up for that. Where'd you hear that story?"

"You saw that it brought you back from your stasis, didn't you?"

"Yeah, and it was really cool of you to do that."

"So, you are now my servants. I am the Master of the Shield!" LePaco screamed.

"Whoa, whoa. Slow down there, guy. You *did* bring us back. We're all pretty thankful for that. Totally A-OK from this lot, no doubt. But all of us did plenty of fighting in our day and we've kind of enjoyed a more peaceful life. If it's all the same, I think we'll all just head out, let you guys figure out what you need to figure out, and we'll be out of your hair. Sound good?"

LePaco's eyes were ablaze. His temples pounded so hard that Duke imagined they could be heard on the Keltian moons.

"No, my dear Grozzel," the admiral said with a strained formality, "you and your friends *will* do my bidding. And my bidding is to kill every one of these pests... now."

Grozzel looked at the battered barrier. The heads of Keltians and members of other races peered over it to see what was happening.

"What'd they do to you, anyways?" the Psitakki asked.

"They're trying to stop me," LePaco replied.

"From what? Universal domination?"

The Psitakki began to laugh. His comrades joined in. LePaco's face turned scarlet.

"Why yes, my Psitakki friend, universal domination *is* my goal."

"Good one, man. Universal domination—oh, that's a good one." Grozzel wiped tears of laughter from his cheek. "I've been so rude. I never asked your name."

"Admiral Lothario LePaco. And this here is my new toy." He raised his forearm, once again producing the combination of blinding light followed by a shockwave.

This again? thought Duke.

Most of the beings hit the floor, though some of the sturdier combatants remained upright from the blow of the Shield's shockwave.

"Hey, what was that for?" one of them yelled.

Grozzel returned to his feet. "What gives, Admiral? Just because we won't fight those folks over there, you're going to try and blind us?"

"That's how this whole 'you will do my bidding' arrangement works," answered LePaco.

"These guys don't look too bad. Are you sure you can't

work something out? You know how many wars could've been avoided if people just talked things out?"

"Kill them now, slaves!" LePaco shouted, raising the inter-dimensional doomsday device.

"Fine, fine," Grozzel said. He pivoted towards his fellow champions. "Hey, guys, wanna just get this over with and then we can leave and not have to deal with this garbage?"

A wave of "fine's" and "why not's" rippled through the group of tournament winners.

Grozzel turned back to the admiral. "Okay, Admiral. We'll do it. It won't be with a lot of enthusiasm, but we'll do it. Then can we go?"

"Sure," LePaco replied, his grin growing even wider.

The ninety-nine warriors stretched, cracked their necks, and limbered up for the impending assault.

"Alright, let's all get into a formation or something," groaned the Timorian. "These guys don't look like much but neither did Nedrow Ostravok, the Cuddle Monster of Daedeaus Maroon. Little did I know that 'cuddling' on Daedeaus Maroon meant slicing one's enemy into dainty ribbons with a huge sickle that Daedeans excrete from a mucus cell in their stomachs. Ned wasn't cuddly at all."

Duke hobbled to the barricade. With his bleeding having abated a little, he vaulted over. His right leg was still injured from the dagger wound to the thigh and couldn't support him on his landing, which turned into more of a tumble and roll. If anything, it was this that caught the attention of Grozzel and his friends.

CHAPTER 30

SAND

G ROZZEL AND THE WARRIORS SHIFTED into their various battle stances.

"Settle down, fellas, I'm not here to fight you," pleaded Duke.

The entire group began to chuckle again.

"We weren't overly concerned with you and the fight you might bring to us," responded Grozzel.

"Although you might be just like Ned from Daedeaus Maroon," noted the Timorian. "Tell me, do you have a mucus-covered sickle in your belly?"

"I don't, I promise," replied the bounty hunter. "But before you lot try and kill us, I do have two things to say."

"Try?"

"Fine, before you *most undoubtedly* kill us."

"Better. Go on," said the Psitakki graciously.

Duke pointed to Admiral LePaco. "First, and I can't stress this enough, that guy you're helping over there, well, he's a bad dude. He wants to take over the universe. All of it. We may not look like much but we're the best shot of preventing that. The big, funky-looking weapon on his wrist—that's no joke. Imprisoning you and your friends for a million cycles is nothing compared to what it can do given free reign. We're talking destroy-the-entire-universe level here."

"He speaks the truth," shouted the Father, as he remained in the clutches of LePaco's guards.

Grozzel glanced at the human then began to scratch his chin in contemplation. Duke saw a few of the other champions doing the same, or what he assumed was an equivalent gesture.

The Psitakki's cephalopodan gaze locked on to Duke again. "And your second point?"

"If you kill me, you'd be killing a fellow winner of the Tournament of the Shield of the Colossal Calamari."

A collective gasp rang out amongst the warriors.

"Is that so?" inquired Grozzel.

"Yes, I'm the last winner. And I'm sure there's a rule against murdering another winner."

"Not to state the obvious, 'Mister Winner,' but you don't *have* the Shield, do you? That guy over there does." The Psitakki nodded his head in the general direction of Admiral LePaco.

"And if you are telling the truth," the Timorian began, "the Tournament must be going downhill. No offense."

"None taken," said Duke, trying to ignore the six-armed alien's disrespectful jab. "He stole the Shield. Ask anyone. Make a quick call to the Grand Shaman. Or to one of your descendants. In fact, a relative of yours named Gjrazzel fought in the event. And did so honorably. He'll tell you the truth."

"Lies! This man is lying!" screamed LePaco.

"And how do we know you're telling the truth?" the Psitakki asked the admiral.

"I have the Shield, don't I?"

"You also tried to kill us with it," countered Grozzel. "So there's that."

"I won the damn tournament! I have the damn Shield. That should be enough proof. Do you think the Psitakki would let some stranger just walk right up and steal it from the champion? Wouldn't a real champion be able to protect a single shield?"

"He has some good points," said the Timorian.

"True, Eux-Auhr-Herx, very true. So, Admiral, tell us about the Tournament. What did it *feel* like to compete?"

LePaco let out a deep sigh. "It was great. I went in there, killed some guys, and claimed my trophy. The Psitakki fans loved me. They said that I reminded them of Grozzel the Great, the first champion of the Tournament of the Shield. There were parades. I don't know... what else... oh yeah, I beat a giant two-headed Jungafallowian that turned out to be a robot."

Grozzel leaned over and said something to Eux-Auhr-Hurx. The Timorian appeared to be in agreement .

"And you, my wounded friend. What did you *feel*?" the Psitakki asked Duke.

Duke closed his eyes. The images from his time on Psitakki raced by, and he tried to pluck out the ones that he thought would be meaningful to the former champions. But the flow of memories was too rapid. He closed his eyes even tighter, trying to tune out the remnants of the battle that surrounded him. He blocked out the images of the ninety-nine warriors staring him down. He blocked out the lingering pain in his thigh from Mazilda's dagger. He did his best to ignore the fact that the most evil being in the known universe was on the other side of the room, wielding a weapon that could send the dimension onto the scrapheap of extinction with the flick of his wrist. Duke let the wave of memories wash over him.

Duke opened his eyes. He looked into the black pupils of the tournament's inaugural champion. He stopped thinking and he simply spoke.

"The sand on the arena floor. I remember the sand. When you walked on it, or pivoted, or dove away from a strike, it was cushioned. But you didn't sink into it, nor did it fight against you. But, when you were thrown from your feet by another's force, it was as solid and painful as any club or rock. It was like it knew if you were deserving of comfort or pain. It had a smell to it too, somewhere between that deep musty smell of wet soil and the sharpness of a salty sea. I felt that it had a mind of its own, it was alive, organic. Somehow it knew the worthiness of the combatants that stood atop it."

The bounty hunter paused to take a deep breath.

"And the crowd. When I was engaged with my opponent, the noise dissipated. It just went away. I knew it was there, somewhere, but I couldn't tell if they were for me or against me. It provided a spark of adrenaline, but also, counter-intuitively, it gave me clarity of mind."

"And your opponents?" asked the Psitakki.

"I hated every second of every fight. I was doing this for what? A Shield? I was hurting other life forms for a trophy? It made me sick. But I kept fighting. The only thing stronger than the illness that the Tournament caused was my desire to win it. For every gut-wrenching moment, there was a smile; for every fleeting instant of joy, there was a sidesplitting sense of agony."

Duke looked up to the ceiling, his eye moistened by tears.

"I see," said Grozzel, his voice cracking.

"You don't believe that garbage," cackled Admiral LePaco. "Really? You can't honestly take that seriously. I have the Shield. I was there. He's just—"

"Admiral, please," interrupted Grozzel. "This man here—"

"Is a liar? A charlatan? An idiot?" interrupted LePaco in turn.

"This man here is a fellow champion. He is a brother."

"And that makes *you* an evil bastard," added the Timorian.

The ninety-nine warriors about-faced to point directly at LePaco and his contingent of Four I's soldiers.

The admiral simply shook his head. "I guess you lot are equally as thick as LaGrange. You could've been my elite guards, my detail; now you'll just be dead."

He tilted his forearm, aiming the device at the champions.

The rebels began to spill over the barricade protecting them from the Four I's assault. They stormed past Duke and joined the ninety-nine warriors, filling in the gaps and creating one sweeping mob, readying themselves for a final charge against LePaco's force. The injured bounty hunter felt a firm, comforting hand on his shoulder.

Thanks, Ish.

Another hand rested on his other shoulder. He turned and exchanged smiles with the beautiful Neprian, Ja'a. Behind her was Lilly, supporting the recovering Queen Joe.

"That was beautiful, what you said, Duke," said Ja'a. "I don't know if I've ever heard you speak like that before."

"I made it up," replied Duke with a smirk. "The sand just felt like... sand."

"You're an ass," said Queen Joe.

"I agree," added Ja'a.

"But I can't think of a better ass to stand beside me at this moment," said Joe.

"I agree with that even more," Ja'a replied.

"That means a lot, don't get me wrong," replied Duke, "but if LePaco figures out how to fire that thing with anything more than light, none of this matters."

It wasn't the Queen or Duke or Lilly that led the charge. A roar from within the ranks of the ninety-nine warriors signaled the advance. But then it was a collective shriek from the combined force that signaled their sudden stop.

A bolt of green energy shot from LePaco's arm, darted over the heads of the rebels, and blasted through the ceiling of Cyborg Joe's. Constant bombardment from an entire armada of battleships couldn't make a dent on the exterior of the famed watering hole, but one whizzing beam of emerald light from the weapon ripped a hole in the ceiling big enough to survey the entirety of the Keltian sky.

The rebels were mostly sprawled out across the barroom floor, many lying on the ground. Admiral LePaco's eyes bulged. The Key, protruding from the Orb, was radiating the same green as the laser. The color then migrated to the Orb itself. Then the Shield.

Joe looked over at Duke, Ishiro'shea, and Ja'a. Her body was trembling; had she not been held in Gartoshian clutches, she would have collapsed.

"It's powering up."

CHAPTER 31

OF PENGUINS AND BLENDERS

"I GUESS THIS IS WHERE I would insert my villainous diatribe of power, right?" said Admiral Lothario LePaco. "But we all know how that sort of thing typically ends."

The weapon on his forearm pulsed rapidly, its glow turning Cyborg Joe's interior a rich shade of green. No color was spared. Even greens became, somehow, greener.

"So, without further ado," he continued, "I'm going to blast you all from the very fabric of this existence and into your inter-dimensional graves. I would say it's been a pleasure and that you put up a good fight, but we all know that wouldn't be an honest assessment. LaGrange, you were pretty much as expected but I did think you, Queenie, would provide more resistance. I guess I didn't realize how powerful I really am."

"For someone that wasn't going to start the clichéd, long-winded bad guy speech, you sure are starting a clichéd, long-winded bad guy speech," jabbed the Nova Texan. "You remind me of your half-brother."

"Are you sure pissing him off is the best approach, Duke?" whispered Lilly.

"Probably not but it's just so natural," answered the bounty hunter.

"Fine, LaGrange, I'll hurry up and get on with killing you and your friends. And I bid you all farewell."

The admiral lowered himself, his legs sprawled out to brace himself against the recoil of the weapon.

"Again, LaGrange, I bid you, the Queen, and everyone else fare—"

The blast came from the opening in the ceiling. It wasn't exceptionally loud, or bright, or green. But it was accurate. It struck LePaco's forearm, forcing the maniacal criminal to the ground. He partially released the weapon, but not before he commanded it to serve up another surge of emerald devastation. Once again, the beam entered the Keltian night sky—this time through the preexisting opening. However, LePaco's fall caused the beam to clip the edges of the gaping hole. And the unknown shooter. Ceiling fragments exploded into the air and tumbled down to the floor of Joe's, bringing with it the heroic warrior that had winged the admiral just as he was about to wipe out the last vestiges of hope for the universe's survival.

The marksman hit the ground unceremoniously, coming to rest amongst the debris. He was sprawled out, motionless and clinging to life.

"Dallas."

Even as Duke's brain raced to digest the situation, LePaco was up, appearing to have shaken off any damage caused by Duke Dallas. He made his way to his feet and soon located the weapon, a few paces away. The admiral reached for it but was tackled by a tiny blur. A tiny blur named Yumi Nobunaga-Flaherty. She had broken free. LePaco regained control rather quickly and threw Ishiro's mother to the ground. But was then met with a slightly larger blur, the Father. He wrapped the admiral in a tight bear hug and flung him to the ground. The Father then pounced on the crazed overlord, fists raining down on the turtled LePaco. It wasn't clear how many of the haymakers were connecting solidly but it probably didn't feel good.

Yumi dove on top of the weapon, acting as a human shield between it and the admiral. She was only slightly larger than the device itself.

The Four I's soldiers came to the aid of LePaco, prying the spry Irishman from their leader. He fell to the floor—landing next to his wife, still guarding the weapon. The admiral drew his pulse pistol and aimed it directly at Ishiro'shea's parents.

"I think you have my weapon," he muttered through gritted teeth, his eyes filled with white-hot fire.

A loud crash rang through Cyborg Joe's. It was the sound that a penguin makes when you put it in a blender—then drop it on a landmine.

Oh, that familiar sound.

Duke LaGrange, Nova Texan bounty hunter and playboy, was holding his beloved out-of-date Widowmaker sonic shotgun. It was aimed where the admiral once stood. But Ol' Betsy made sure that the admiral was no longer able to stand. In fact, he was no longer able to do anything that had the prerequisite of being alive. Duke LaGrange had just killed Admiral Lothario LePaco.

Time seemed to stand still; ages seemed to pass.

It was the Hilterian ambassador, Lutra, who broke the silence, shouting, "Let's go!"

Grozzel; Eux-Auhr-Herx; the ninety-seven other past champions of the Tournament of the Shield of the Colossal Calamari; Lilly, the anthropomorphic musk ox from one of the moons of Gartosh; Lutra, the Hilterian sharpshooter; and Gha, a feisty Goother Rat from Gurlf joined a mix of Keltian freedom fighters and other alien volunteers and charged the disciplined squadron from Intergalactic Infrastructure Improvement, Incorporated.

The Four I's soldiers attempted to flee outside of Cyborg Joe's—but were cut off by even more Keltian defenders, a legion of Hausen-Ra, Gartoshians, Sabromms, and other species that had just taken out the remainder of LePaco's ground force. Hovering in the air above, visible through the gaping hole in the ceiling, was the *Deus Ex Machina*, flanked by the victorious fleet of Earth and Gartoshian ships, led by Maxx Gemstarr.

The Four I's were overwhelmed.

Duke rushed to the pile of debris that covered his father. He began to cast away fragments of wood and stone with the strength of eight T'ckuvians. Ja'a joined him. The amount of debris left in the wake of the weapon's blast was enough to bury an entire colony of three-headed ice wombats. The duo soon cleared away enough to make out a humanoid form.

Duke continued digging until a face looked back at him. And though he'd only seen that face for the first time in adulthood a short while ago, it was part of him. It was his DNA. It was a mirror into his future. It was his father.

"Dad, Dad!" Duke screamed. "Can you hear me?"

"Now you call me Dad?" said Dallas faintly with the slight hint of a grin on his battered face.

"How did you—Why?" the bounty hunter stammered.

"Stop, Lafayette. Stop. I don't have much time."

"We're going to get you out of here," Duke pleaded.

"Stop. Please, stop." He looked to Ja'a. "Pretty lady. Tell him to stop, please."

The Neprian clasped Duke's hand tightly, her other hand gripped his forearm.

"We can get you out—"

"Lafayette, stop and listen to me. I'm dying. So shut up and let me talk."

Duke tried to fight back his emotions. His jaw quivered and his vision grew blurry as salty tears burst from his eyes.

"I'm glad that I sent you back. I know you had a hand in this."

"How'd you survive the attack back on Tardasio 5?"

"Most of us survived. Who knew that BHU and organized crime could work so well together. Maybe a little too well. But we did the opposite of what everyone predicted. When our backs were against the wall after that sneak attack, we fought harder. We laid waste to that entire planet. The Four I's won't be able to produce a construction paper hand turkey with what we left. Then I got a message from a guy claiming to be your best friend. A guy named Maxx."

"Maxx, he's a—Never mind, it doesn't matter."

"He said you'd say something like that."

"However you got here, thank you for saving me. For saving us."

"It's the best that I could do, Duke. I spent my entire life *not* doing the best that I could do, with you in particular. I'll never be able to make that up."

Duke Dallas' voice trembled and he began to cough. A single stream of blood fell from the corner of his mouth. "I never planned on it being like this, but I should tell you about your mother. I owe you that."

"No need, Dad, I knew my mother. She died a long time ago on Nova Texas."

A river of tears cascaded down Dallas' cheek and washed away much of the blood.

"Trix *was* a great woman. I wish you would've had more time with her, Son. I really do." He paused. "But, if you do want to find your *biological* mother, I would start your search on Omarellia. I don't know if she's still there or if she still answers to 'Juni,' or even if she's alive, but that's where I would start. But beware... You probably don't want to know. If it were up to me—and I know it's not—I would leave it alone. But it's not and you deserve the right to make that decision, despite what I say."

"Thank you," replied the bounty hunter. "Thank you."

"And one last thing, Son. I know I don't deserve a last

request but if you can find it in your heart, I would appreciate it."

"Yes, anything," stammered Duke.

"Bury me. Bury me on a planet that's—" He stopped, his coughing increasing.

His lungs are filling with blood, concluded Duke.

"Yes, Father."

"A planet that's peaceful. I've only known violence. War. Criminal activity. The death of innocent beings. Bury me on a place that has moved beyond war and death. Or one that wants to. Somewhere untouched by guys like LePaco and criminals like Hefty."

Ja'a strengthened her grip on Duke's arm and rested her head on his shoulder.

"I know the place," Duke said. "You'll love it. Sweeping plains dotted with glass-like ponds. Majestic mountains like you've never seen, protecting vast valleys. And you'll get a kick out of this: they have winged panthers flying around everywhere. There are swamps, full of life and diversity. There are forests, dense forests. And caves... Oh, are there caves."

"What's the name of this paradise?" asked Duke Dallas, his voice reduced to a whisper.

"They call it Neprius."

"It sounds wonderful, Son. It sounds—" Duke Dallas' voice trailed off as his last breath exited his body.

"It's wonderful, Dad. I once thought it was nothing but a primitive, backwards world. But now I know it's the most beautiful place in the whole universe."

As Duke sat motionless on the pile of rubble, he noticed Ishiro'shea race to his parents. The ninja removed the mouth covering on his mask and the recognition was instant. All three burst into tears as they embraced. Despite the emotional ordeal that he had just experienced, Duke smiled.

Just next to the feet of the reunited family, still glowing a radioactive green, were the Key, Orb, and Shield. The hobbled Queen Joe made her way to the trio and extended a firm hand to Ishiro'shea's parents. She hugged the ninja with as much emotion as his own parents did. Ishiro'shea picked up the weapon and handed it to the Queen.

She closed her eyes. From around her hands, the obsidian smoke that typically signified one of her stormy lightning assaults began to fill the air. It formed into winding tubes, weaving around the weapon. The intensity of the artifacts' glow faded until they appeared inert and harmless.

Joe fell to the ground, dropping the weapon. The three artifacts broke apart, scattering to encircle the inter-dimensional being lying on the floor of her bar.

She exhaled deeply, as if she had been holding in her breath for an eon.

CHAPTER 32

ANOTHER ROUND OF WHISKY

"WE CAUGHT THIS ONE TRYING to escape," said Grozzel the Great, holding up a battered Mazilda Cloax by the neck, her feet dangling in the air. "I think she just woke up. What should we do with her?"

"Just kill me, you bastards," she said through cracked lips matted with dried blood.

A bruise extended from her ear, across the bridge of her nose, and halfway down her opposite cheek. Grozzel poked it with his long cephalopodan finger. The assassin writhed in pain. The Psitakki giggled. "She's feisty."

"Duke, thoughts?" asked Queen Joe. "I feel that this is your call."

"What's your plan, Grozzel? Where are you guys headed now?" asked the bounty hunter.

"We all discussed it and the only place that we'd feel at home is Psitakki. Some of us have been away for a million cycles. Having the arena and the Psitakki people there will help to ease our transition, we think."

"I'm sure we'll be celebrities," added Eux-Auhr-Herx, his chest puffed out and his chin aloft.

"Most definitely," concluded Duke. "How about you guys take her?"

"To Psitakki?" blurted out the Queen.

"Yeah, there's a Chief Interrogator General that will know what to do with her," said the bounty hunter. "Just tell him that Duke LaGrange said to be as creative as possible."

"Sounds fun," replied Grozzel. "We'll do it. And, if I haven't said it already, it was nice meeting you, Duke LaGrange. Now we know all one hundred victors. I don't think we ever thought this day would come. It's provided some much needed closure for us."

Duke removed his hat and placed it against his chest. "I'm humbled to have met all of you. Thank you for your help and for trusting us."

"You made a compelling case with your speech. Very compelling. It sent chills up and down my old spine."

Duke smiled and shook the Psitakki's hand.

He then approached his former love. Mazilda's gaze, even with one eye swollen, was harsh. She opened her mouth but Duke closed it with his finger. She didn't fight back.

"No, you're done talking," he said. "I knew I had bad taste in women. Like really bad. Epically bad. But I thought you were different. I beat myself up, over and over and over for cycles, for letting you go; wondering how different my life would've been with you in it. And I was right to think you were different. You were *worse* than anyone else that I'd ever met. Way worse. Goodbye, Mazilda."

The bounty hunter kissed her on the cheek, putting just enough pressure on the bruise that it caused Mazilda to cringe in pain.

Duke turned to Ja'a, who had been watching the exchange curiously, and flashed her a wink.

"You are awful at picking women, Duke LaGrange," she said.

"What does that say about you?"

Queen Joe was sitting at the bar. The three inter-dimensional artifacts rested on the counter before her.

It's odd seeing the Queen sitting down on one of her own barstools, thought Duke.

Behind the bar, Earl was sorting through the damaged goods, broken bottles, and cracked shelving. The battle had taken its toll on Cyborg Joe's inventory.

The surviving Four I's soldiers that hadn't managed to escape had been rounded up by the Bounty Hunters Union for imprisonment or to be taken to one of the many galactic crime lords for their own unique brand of discipline. And those were the lucky ones. Some were thrown in ships and sent to Earth to be punished as war criminals by the Irish and Japanese.

Many of the Keltians remained at Joe's, sweeping, dusting, and beginning the long road of restoring the bar to its former glory. Po'l and Ja'a joined them, clearing out the bodies of the deceased and other even less savory remnants of combat—reminiscing all the while.

It's good seeing them back together, talking about Neprius, thought Duke. *It has to mean a lot for both of them.*

Duke was helping Ishiro'shea and his parents turn over a booth that had been flipped during the altercation with LePaco's forces when the Queen stood up. She whispered something to Earl, who shot back a perplexed stare. He then turned and started to fumble around behind the bar. In record time, he whipped up a martini. Duke recognized *that* martini. It was the Queen's signature cocktail. She took a sip and closed her eyes. They opened. She grabbed Earl's furry paw with both of her hands and squeezed. She leaned over and kissed the Glyptodian on the cheek.

Duke could only just make out her words: "That was perfect, Earl. Just like that, every time."

She then said something else to the hulking barkeep and he returned to digging for something under the counter. He resurfaced with two large bottles of Earth whisky. He set a dozen or so glasses on the bar top. They were a hodgepodge of sizes, colors, shapes, and levels of brokenness. He filled them up to their respective brims.

"Everyone, could you please stop for a second?" Joe requested. She wasn't shouting or even talking loudly, but her words seemed to reach everyone's ears as if she was screaming into them from an eyelash's length away.

Everyone stopped, then began to encircle the proprietor of Cyborg Joe's.

The Queen began. "After millions of cycles in this dimension and the last stretch right here on this wonderful planet of Kelt, in this wonderful bar, with the *mostly* wonderful creatures of this universe, it's now time for me to return."

An outburst of shock and defiance poured from her loyal followers and patrons.

"This isn't negotiable, friends," she continued. "I want to stay, but you all know that I can't. Someone has to rid this universe of these things." She gestured at the three artifacts. "And it *has* to be me."

It was an open and shut case. She was the only inter-dimensional being amongst them, the only one capable of securely depositing these weapons somewhere out of the reach of any member of the universe.

"Thank you all for understanding."

"What are you going to do, Queen? *How* are you going to do it?" asked Lilly.

"The portals that I controlled for cycles at the bar—I'm going to channel them all. But I'm going to summon them all simultaneously. They should be able to create a bubble between the realities of two dimensions—I'm not sure which, but two. I will remain there, with these three items, for what you would call eternity."

"You won't be able to leave?" asked Po'l.

"I won't, my Neprian friend," she said, looking down, "but don't fret. I've had enough good company to fill infinite lifetimes. It's not a sacrifice, it's just what has to be done."

"That seems like a pretty heavy cost, Queen," said Lutra.

Joe opened her mouth but stopped as Duke stepped in front of her.

"Anything without a cost isn't worth having, right?" he said.

The Queen chuckled and put her hand on Duke's shoulder.

"Yes, and don't ever forget that, Duke LaGrange."

The bounty hunter yanked her from her barstool and wrapped both arms around her. "Thank you, Queen Joe. Thank you for everything."

Cyborg Joe's was filled with cheers and platitudes regarding the Queen and her bar.

Po'l cleared his throat. "Excuse me, Queen. Not to be insensitive, but what about the bar? Does this mean the end of the bar too?"

Joe looked back at Earl and nodded. "Earl's martinis are virtually indistinguishable from mine," she proclaimed.

The rebels let out a primal cheer in celebration of this good news.

"So you gave it to Earl?" asked Po'l.

"No, Mister Po'l," the Glyptodian bellowed. "I am not the new owner and manager of Cyborg Joe's... However, I have been told that my services as bartender and concierge at Cyborg Joe's will be retained."

"Cheers to that," replied Duke.

"Then who owns it?" asked the Neprian expat.

A head seemed to pop up from behind the bar, an arm's length from Earl. It was a handsome face, youthful and vibrant. His eyes were a twinkling sable, his skin tawny beige. His auburn hair was cut short, but still appeared messy.

No one seemed to immediately recognize this mysterious newcomer. Even Duke was forced to do a double-take.

"You're giving Cyborg Joe's to Ishiro?" asked the bounty hunter.

Queen Joe's smile was so intense that Duke imagined he could fit his entire finger in one of her dimples.

"We just saved the universe with that space ninja right there, so why can't we save Cyborg Joe's with a space ninja?" said Joe.

"Don't you mean a *drunk* space ninja?" asked Ishiro'shea in a rich and honeyed tone. He downed one of the glasses of whisky that Earl had placed on the counter.

The mob let loose a cavalcade of praise upon the new owner as they made their way to the bar to partake in the celebratory liquor.

"So, little buddy," Duke began, "after all these cycles, that's what your voice sounds like?"

"Is it what you thought it would sound like?" asked Ishiro'shea.

"A little underwhelmed, if I'm being honest. Maybe it's an acquired taste," Duke responded, a sly smirk on his face.

"Well, now you know what I've felt like for all this time."

The bounty hunter's grin grew; he nodded to his best friend and partner and tossed the whisky down his throat.

Out of the corner of his eye, in the distance, he saw a flash of crimson light.

She's gone.

CHAPTER 33

WELCOME TO CYBORG JOE'S... AGAIN

T HE CROWD SLOWLY POURED INTO Cyborg Joe's Grill N' Go & The Why Not Saloon. Given that it had only narrowly escaped destruction, along with the end of the universe, a week earlier, the steady flow of patrons was quite impressive. But the all-new Joe's already had a loyal customer base. Ishiro'shea and team had successfully repaired the ceiling, patching the gaping hole caused by a stray blast from the inter-dimensional doomsday device. Most of the original signs had been rehung, their neon no less vibrant than before they were knocked off the wall during the firefight between the Queen's forces and those of the sinister Admiral LePaco. The floors were even clean—for Cyborg Joe's, that is. The clientele sported a few more locals than normal and, even though the bar's previous main attraction—the Queen's portals —were gone, the atmosphere and buzz remained intact. The kitchen was pumping out MechaBurger 8000s as fast as Earl was mixing *his* famous martinis.

But behind the bar, greeting customers, new and old alike, wasn't an enigmatic inter-dimensional goddess with a sharp wit only matched by her pansophical wisdom. Instead, there was a stout and exuberant man from Earth, a skilled warrior from one of the most violence-riddled planets in the galaxy but who had a caring heart that embraced all. He spoke little, but what he said spoke volumes. In some ways, he was the only one that could have taken over Cyborg Joe's after Queen Joe left the dimension to stow away the three artifacts that almost brought an end to everyone. It was the happiest that Duke had ever seen his long-time friend, Ishiro'shea.

"I still can't believe I'm here," Yeop said to Duke. "One second I'm grieving over Master Ishiro, the next I'm in a space battle, and now I'm at Cyborg Joe's. *The* Cyborg Joe's. No one's going to believe me back home."

"Cheers, Yeop. And thanks again," said Duke, lifting his glass in a toast.

"My fellow Gartoshians spoke very highly of your tactics in the battle, my new tiny Earth friend," said Lilly as she raised her glass of Glytopdian Summer Ale. "Some unorthodox moves that they've never seen before."

Yeop blushed. "Thanks, Lilly. I'm going to miss you guys when I go back to Earth," he said with a frown.

"At least you don't have to go back to Gurlf," replied Po'l.

Gha, the Goother rat, spun around on his stool and sneered at the Neprian. "At least our swamps don't have flesh-eating cannibals," he fired back.

"They have worse. They have *your* relatives," said Po'l.

Liquor was expelled from Gha's nose like flames from a blowtorch. He lost his balance and fell to the floor. "You win this round, Po'l," he chuckled as he climbed back onto his stool. "Well played."

"Indeed," added Lutra in a sultry tone as she draped her arms around Po'l's neck and chest from behind. "And if you keep playing well... Well, who knows." She planted a peck on Po'l's cheek.

"Watch out for her, Po'l," Duke began, "Hilterian women are—"

"They're what?" interjected Ja'a.

"They're to be treated with respect," finished the bounty hunter with a wry grin. "That's all I was going to say."

Ja'a burst into laughter. The rest of the patrons followed suit.

"You've got jokes now?" Duke asked Ja'a. "When did this happen?"

She playfully slapped him on the leg. "You try and run a planetary government. It speeds up the development of one's sense of humor."

"Seriously though, everyone," said the Nova Texan, "if I can make a toast, I would just like to offer cheers to Queen Joe!"

They all raised their glasses to the former owner.

Duke continued, "And to her formidable replacement, a Salutatorian no less, Ishiro'shea Nobunaga-Flaherty!"

They all raised their glasses even higher to the current owner. The ninja blushed.

"You're still paying for those drinks," said Ishiro'shea.

A chorus of playful boos rained down on him.

"So, Ishiro'shea, where are your parents?" asked Lilly. "I haven't seen them the last few days."

"They went back to Earth to try and pick up the broken pieces and start humanity down a different path," replied the bar owner. "It will be difficult, but they were both looking forward to the challenge. They were happy to be going home."

Ishiro dropped down below the bar and pulled out three unique bottles and a short cubical glass. He mixed the liquids quickly but carefully, then slid the glass to the Gartoshian. "Lilly, I wanted you to try this first."

The anthropomorphic musk ox took a hearty sip. Then another.

"This is delicious," she said, taking in another gulp of the creamy beverage. "What's in it?"

"The base is Earth vodka. The Earth ships left some for us before they went back home. I mixed it with Gartoshian Snow

Juice. Some of your brethren donated some to the bar before they departed to Gartosh. It's an elegantly sweet liqueur; I can't believe I hadn't discovered it earlier. Lastly, a splash of a secret ingredient."

"Let me taste that," said Duke, swiping the glass from Lilly and finishing off the drink. He swished it around in his mouth, letting the flavorful cocktail touch every taste bud. "Holy hedgehogs, you bastard. I know that 'secret' ingredient. It's the damn icing on Aintin Kuniko's Irish whisky cakes. It has to be. How did you pull that off?"

Ishiro'shea nodded at Yeop.

"Hey, I never leave Earth without stashing away a few boxes in my ship," replied Yeop. "And now I have a reason to come back; Ishiro'shea will need a constant supply if this drink's going to be as popular as I think it'll be."

He's a pretty smart kid, surmised Duke.

"What are you calling this new concoction, Ish?" asked the bounty hunter.

"It's called the Yvonne."

Lilly lowered her head.

I've never seen her like this, thought Duke.

"A worthy name, indeed," said Duke, raising the empty glass to the sky.

"What's a worthy name?"

Not that voice. Please not that voice.

"What'd I miss, guys?" asked Maxx Gemstarr. "It doesn't matter; what matters is that I'm here now and the partying can begin."

He slapped Duke hard on the back. It hurt.

"How to ruin a moment, courtesy of Maxx Gemstarr, everybody," said Duke.

"C'mon, what's cooking around here—" Maxx paused and turned to Ja'a. "Easy answer: it's you."

He extended his hand to the Neprian. She shook it.

"I'm Maxx Gemstarr, the Universe's Favorite Bounty Hunter. And you are?"

"Ja'a. From Neprius."

"Neprius? Never heard of it. How about a drink?"

"I'm good. Duke keeps me pretty liquored up."

Maxx's brow furrowed. "*That* Duke?"

"Yes, *that* Duke."

"Yes, *this* Duke," said the Nova Texan, pointing to himself.

"I'm sorry, best buddy o' mine, I keep underestimating you. But I do have some good news to share."

"We can't wait," said Duke unenthusiastically.

"I've talked it over with Mama Fong and I'm taking on the role of President of the Bounty Hunters Union. She's retiring to Oscavia."

"What's the good news?" smirked Duke.

"What are you talking about? I—Maxx Gemstarr, the bounty hunter's bounty hunter, Mr. Popular, Everyone's Favorite—am going to be the new BHU president. How awesome is that?"

"I've now officially seen it all. Astral anomalies, magic orbs, and Jungafallowian androids have nothing on this," stated Duke. "But congrats are in order. Ish, pour this man a drink."

Ishiro'shea slid a nearly full glass of Erontian saké to Maxx. He chugged it, almost gagging on the potent blast of fermented fury.

"It gets even better," Gemstarr said in between coughs. "I'm moving the BHU headquarters from Daedeaus Purple as my first order of business."

"Where to, dare I ask?" inquired Duke.

"Right next door. We're going to be neighbors, Ish."

The ninja slammed down an equally full glass of Erontian saké.

The *Deus Ex Machina* looked as grand as it ever had. Grand in the broad sense of the word, of course. Its shadow engulfed both bounty hunters standing beneath its battle-scarred hull.

"Hard to believe you aren't coming aboard, little buddy," said Duke. "I'm not sure the ship's going to like that. You were always her favorite."

Ishiro'shea didn't say anything, he just embraced his bounty hunting companion.

"If you ever need me, I know you'll find a way to get ahold of me. If anyone can, it's you," said the Nova Texan.

"And if you ever need me—or a well-made martini—I know you'll find a way back here," replied the ninja. He dropped his head and took in a deep breath. "I want to apologize, Duke."

"You? Apologize? For all the crap that *I've* put you through, I don't think *you* need to apologize."

"Seriously. I was selfish for this vow of silence. Think of all of the times that we could have escaped or I could have warned—"

"Ish, shut up. You might not have spoken, but you always said a ton. Don't ever apologize for that again."

Ishiro'shea extended his hand. Duke gripped it tightly and covered both of their hands with his free one.

"It's been beyond a pleasure getting into the scraps we did across this fair universe. We picked up women, we won at pit fighting, and now we saved the universe. And we found your parents. I think that was the most rewarding thing that we've ever done."

"And *your* father too," Ishiro'shea reminded Duke.

"Speaking of my father, I should probably go. I have a deceased father in the ship's deep freeze, waiting to be buried after all. I don't want him to thaw out—and I'm not really sure how long this sliver of Orb will even last. It doesn't look like it has that much juice, but I'm done predicting anything related to magical rocks. The Queen didn't give us any directions, she just said it would be enough to get Ja'a back home."

"That's probably a good idea," replied Ishiro'shea. "When you get to Neprius, say hi to Uu'k for me. Make sure she keeps up with those lessons. She could be a damn good swordswoman if she sticks to it."

"I will," Duke said. He released Ishiro'shea's hand and turned to the *Deus*. After a few steps, he spun around.

"This is just crazy, isn't it? You running Cyborg Joe's... and *talking*. Me carrying back my biological father's frozen body to be buried on Neprius. Ja'a. The Queen. Mazilda. Maxx. I never thought a day like this would ever happen. I never thought we'd be standing here today."

"I did," the ninja said with a wink and a big thumbs-up.

CHAPTER 34

THAT PRIMITIVE ROCK

DUKE KNELT AMONGST THE VAST expanse of vegetation in the valley, an endless sea of flax, jade, and white. The rocky cliffs that formed a sky-piercing perimeter around the grassland were as majestic as Duke remembered. He scanned the cloudless sky, his eyes jumping from one to another of the tiny winged silhouettes dancing across the blue tapestry. He closed his eyes and could hear the celebratory purrs of the grundar fighting through the gentle valley breeze. There were no signs of bloodshed or struggle or violence. If Duke had been tasked with explaining what "tranquil" meant to a new species, this vista would be his entry.

He placed a polished stone on a patch of soil, marking the unadorned grave. He pressed and turned it until it was firmly embedded into the soft dirt.

It read: *Here lies Duke H. Dallas. Gunslinger. Ship Captain. Booze Man. Father.*

He stood up and tried his best to soak in all of the beauty that surrounded him. He removed his hat and let the Neprian sun beat down upon him, feeling each ray permeate his skin. The sweet smell of the valley's grass swirled around his nostrils. He inhaled, filling his lungs with its effervescent aroma.

"Hey," said Ja'a, tugging on his arm. "Are you okay?"

Duke turned to look at her. She was still as stunning as the day he had first seen her in the cave. It seemed like so long ago.

"Yes," he replied, "the best I've ever felt."

"Are you sure? You could have stayed with Ishiro'shea and the bar." She stared at the ground. "I would have made sure your father was buried properly."

"Ja'a, I didn't *want* to stay. I want to be here, with you."

He grabbed her chin gently, lifting her head until their eyes met. He kissed her.

"We can always go back," said the Neprian.

"You're kinda in charge of this planet, remember?" Duke jabbed. "I don't think you can just pick up and go on a vacation to Kelt on a whim. Besides, there's not a warp station within a lifetime's voyage that we know about, even in a ship as impressive as the *Deus*."

"True."

"And, in case you forgot, this is all we have left of Queen Joe's present."

Duke extended his hand, his fingers daintily pinching a strand of twine. The twine, in turn, supported a leathery purse no bigger than Duke's fist. He emptied its contents into his other hand, open and facing the sky. Out poured a stream of sand, rocky and metallic, forming a tiny mound in the bounty hunter's palm.

"This is the last of any magic orbs that we'll ever have to see again."

"And your ticket home," Ja'a added.

Duke grinned and, with one massive exhalation, blew the pile of ground-up Orb into the gentle breeze of the Valley of the Grundar.

"This is my home," he said.

Ja'a gave Duke another kiss.

"We should probably get going if we're going to make it to Sansagon tonight. I know the grundar are fast but I don't want to be late."

Why didn't we take the Deus *again?* thought Duke.

"It would be rude for us to be late," Ja'a continued. "Plus, Vernglet is so eager to hear about your escapades. He won't stop asking me about them. And I'm making soufflés tonight. I think I've mastered them, finally."

Happiness overcame the bounty hunter. *Finally.*

"I'll meet you back at the grundar. Can I have a few more moments with my dad?"

Ja'a squeezed his hand and headed back to the edge of the valley where their winged feline transportation awaited to take them to Sansagon.

Duke looked down at his father's headstone. "I wish you could've been on some of Ish's and my adventures. You woulda loved 'em, Dad. Women, whisky, and weaponry. We had this one trick, it always worked. I would say 'Have you ever seen someone cut off their own head...' Never mind, you had to be there, I guess." The bounty hunter sighed. "We did some good, though. I don't know if I woulda always made you proud but, then again, you weren't exactly perfect either. I know, I know, water under the bridge. You *did* save my life and, kinda, the universe, so I'll give you a pass on the leaving-me-when-I-was-a-kid thing. But, seriously, I wish you woulda been there. You woulda loved Ish too. I had the best friend a degenerate loudmouth bounty hunter could've ever had. And he was the damn Salutatorian. I really hope that I can make it on my own without him. And Queen Joe, for that matter. I don't know how the universe is going to make it without her. But, as long as Cyborg Joe's is around, the universe has a fighting chance."

He looked up into the Neprian sky again. "I finally found someone that makes me think about someone other than myself... and I'm fairly confident that she won't align herself with a maniacal overlord bent on universal domination. At least I hope not. That wouldn't happen twice to the same person, would it? I think you'd approve of Ja'a. And if you didn't, she'd probably beat your ass. She's like no one else I've ever met. And apparently, she's moving her entire race into the 'soufflé stage.' Impressive, right?" Duke took in another breath of fresh Neprian air. "Holy hedgehogs, I nearly forgot. The news of what you did reached Hefty Senchax. He was so moved that he named his ship, a bar, and a casino after you. I think he even petitioned to change the name of T'ckuvu Prime to T'ckuvu Duke. If it happens, I'll make sure to come out here and tell ya'."

The bounty hunter wiped the newly formed tears from his cheeks. "Anyways, I gotta go now. The Shepherd of the Grundar, Fazeek, said that he'd watch over you. You'll be able to rest here for as long as you need." He removed his hat and put it over his heart. "Rest easy, Duke Dallas. Enjoy Neprius. It's a good home."

The bounty hunter walked back to Ja'a and the pair of winged panthers waiting restlessly. Ja'a handed Duke the reins and he vaulted himself onto the back of his grundar. A coordinated combination of the flapping of the creatures' powerful wings and the propulsion from their muscular hindquarters thrust the duo into the sky. After another flap, they had cleared the valley ridge and were high above the northern land mass of Neprius.

"You know, Ja'a, I just had an idea," said Duke.

"What's that?"

"I think I'm going to open up a bar. Cyborg Joe's, Neprius branch. I doubt the franchise fees would be that much. Ish would probably cut me a deal. And you can probably help me fast-track some real estate for it."

Ja'a shook her head with a smile, gave the reins a tug, and her grundar accelerated out in front of Duke and his steed.

"Fine. We can table it for now, honey," he shouted.

Ja'a did not turn around.

The bounty hunter closed his eyes and let the wind splash against his face as he darted through the dimming Neprian sky.

He began humming the Nova Texan Planetary Anthem.

THE END

THANK YOU

I hope that you enjoyed *How to Save the Universe with a Drunk Space Ninja*. If so, I'd love for you to join my newsletter at DukeLaGrange.com.

Stay tuned for the continued Adventures of Duke LaGrange!

ABOUT THE AUTHOR

©JAY KEY 2018

JAY KEY knew at a young age that he wanted to be the world's first professional wrestler turned fraternity president turned digital media executive turned Society of Vertebrate Paleontology-approved blog writer turned science-fiction comedy author. At various points, Key called Dallas, San Francisco, and Los Angeles home—but it wasn't until a move to Chicago that writing professionally became a reality. Authoring a serialized version of *The Adventures of Duke LaGrange* and a popular blog on the paleobiological accuracy of dinosaurs in pop culture, Key used that momentum to complete *How to Pick Up Women with a Drunk Space Ninja* in 2017. It debuted with Star Wheel Books in 2018.

Jay now lives in a suburb of Dallas-Fort Worth with his wife, Shelley, their daughter, Finley, and their French bulldog, Olive. He is a member of the Science Fiction & Fantasy Writers of America.

facebook.com/starwheelbooks

twitter.com/ofamesozoicmind

instagram.com/jaykkey